Henrietta
with Louie
from
for Christma~   ~58

Henrietta

THREE JAYS ON HOLIDAY

PAT SMYTHE

Three Jays on Holiday

THE THIRD ADVENTURE OF THE THREE JAYS

With five line-drawings by
J. E. McConnell

CASSELL · LONDON

CASSELL & COMPANY LTD
35 RED LION SQUARE, LONDON, W.C.I

and at

210 Queen Street, Melbourne; 26/30 Clarence Street, Sydney; 24 Wyndham Street, Auckland; 1068 Broadview Avenue, Toronto 6; P.O. Box 275, Cape Town; P.O. Box 11190, Johannesburg; Haroon Chambers, South Napier Road, Karachi; 13/14 Ajmeri Gate Extension, New Delhi 1; 15 Graham Road, Ballard Estate, Bombay 1; 17 Chittaranjan Avenue, Calcutta 13; P.O. Box 23, Colombo; Denmark House, 84 Ampang Road (3rd Floor), Kuala Lumpur; Avenida 9 de Julho 1138, São Paulo; Galeria Güemes, Escritorio 454/59 Florida 165, Buenos Aires; Marne 5b, Mexico 5, D.F.; Sanshin Building, 6 Kanda Mitoschiro-cho, Chiyoda-ku, Tokyo; 25 rue Henri Barbusse, Paris 5e; 25 Ny Strandvej, Espergaerde, Copenhagen; Beulingstraat 2, Amsterdam-C; Bederstrasse 51, Zürich 2

First published 1958

Set in 13-on-14 pt. Bembo type and
printed in Great Britain by
Wyman & Sons Ltd., London, Reading and Fakenham

F.658

AUTHOR'S NOTE

Not long ago, the editor of a well-known children's newspaper rang up to arrange a get-together at Miserden. During the conversation he asked whether the Three Jays would be present! Sadly, I had to tell him that the only place where the Three Jays can be met is in the pages of this and other books in the series.

On the other hand, the backgrounds are authentic and the island of Gallinara does indeed exist, as every visitor to Alassio will confirm. But the existence of treasure there and how it came to be left are 'all my own work'. I would not want any keen readers wasting their breath in diving for treasure that only resides in my own imagination! The villain of my story and his predecessor, the German commander, are completely fictitious and have not been based on real people, either alive or dead.

Finally, I would like to dedicate this third Three Jays adventure to my publishers, Cassell & Company Limited, without whose enthusiastic encouragement and practical help I should never have been able to embark on the series.

Miserden   PAT SMYTHE

CONTENTS

CHAPTER I

Two Letters for Jacky

IT was breakfast time at Miserden House. These stories of mine always seem to open with a meal in progress but that is not surprising. The Three Jays are such hearty eaters that when they are not out riding they usually manage to keep their strength up by getting hold of 'nourishment' in some form or other.

For the benefit of new readers, I must first of all introduce the Three Jays, so called because their names each begin with a J—Jimmy, Jane and Jacky. Jimmy and Jane are brother and sister, second cousins of mine whose father lives in Kenya. They are both at school in Cheltenham, about ten miles away, and they spend their holidays and free week-ends at Miserden. Jacky—or Jacqueline de Vere Field, to give her full name—is no relation of the others. Her father is a very wealthy businessman in London, a widower, and she is his only child. When she first came to Miserden, she was spoilt and conceited but she quickly learned that the size of one's parent's bank balance cut no ice with a frisky pony. She and the other two became the best of friends and formed their exclusive club for three members only.

A stranger suddenly coming across the Three Jays

might easily mistake them for deadly enemies because they are constantly arguing and teasing one another. If you have ever heard the raucous screaming noise that real jays make when they meet in a tree, you will realize the second good reason why my young friends got their nickname.

At the time this present story opens, Jacky's father had just been involved in a plane-crash in America where he was on business. Luckily, he had escaped with only a dislocated shoulder but it had been a most anxious time for all of us, in particular Jacky, until the good news came through by cable. Four days had passed since then and here were the Jays just finishing breakfast, having gallantly fought their way through mountainous helpings of cornflakes, followed by bacon, eggs, toast and marmalade.

I was just drinking a final cup of coffee and said in a mock-sympathetic tone, 'Are you all quite sure you've had enough? I hate to see you going hungry. How about you, Jimmy? Couldn't you manage a side of beef as well? Or perhaps we could arrange to roast an ox in case you need a snack.'

'Ha-ha—funny joke,' was Jimmy's mumbled reply as he crammed half a slice of thickly buttered toast and marmalade into his mouth.

'I suspect she's extracting the Michael, Jim,' said his sister. 'Bad sign when our cousin starts begrudging us food.'

'I'm thinking of the ponies,' I said. 'Having to

carry fat lumps like you. You'd better hold your breath over the jumps in the paddock this morning to get you airborne. If you land heavily with all that breakfast inside you, the poor ponies will have their backs broken!'

Before Jimmy and Jane had time to work out a crushing retort, Paddy, my secretary and one of the mainstays of Miserden House, walked into the dining room with a large bundle of letters in her hand. 'Morning, Pat,' she said. 'And good morning to you, you three young horrors.'

Their mouths being too full to answer, the three young horrors had to be content with just glaring at her. Paddy went on, holding up the bunch of letters, 'The usual thing, Pat. Nothing very urgent as far as I can see. Oh, there are a couple for Jacky. Here you are,' and she dropped them beside Jacky's plate.

Jane had managed to swallow her last mouthful. 'Strange,' she murmured, 'very strange. Who could be writing to Jacky? Everyone knows she can't read.'

'She likes collecting the stamps,' cut in Jimmy. 'She pretends to read what's inside and then throws the letter away when no one's looking.'

Jacky took no notice of their teasing. She had quickly spotted the red and blue stripes on the edges of one envelope, the typical markings of an air mail letter from America. She guessed it must be from or about her father and she ripped it open and began

[3]

reading avidly. After a moment, she looked up, doubt and hope mingling in her shining eyes.

'Oh, Pat,' she half yelled, 'it's a wonderful idea—if we can manage it.'

'Now take a deep breath, Jacky,' I replied, 'and collect your wits. What's wonderful—and what are the snags?'

'It's from Daddy,' she rushed on. 'They're discharging him from hospital but the doctors say the crash may have given him a delayed shock. They want him to cut short his business trip and get away for a good rest. So he's cabled the skipper of his yacht and told him to stock it up and then sail it round Spain to Cannes in the South of France. Daddy's just going to make one or two important calls and then he'll fly direct from New York to Nice, he says, and spend a week or so on the yacht. He wants all of us to join him there!'

This was too good an opportunity for the other two to miss. 'Cannes,' murmured Jane. 'Well, if he can, we can!'

Before the rest of us could shriek with horror at the atrocious pun, Jimmy said, 'That'll be very Nice—I mean, nice.'

'Steady on,' I pleaded. 'It's a bit early in the day for that kind of humour.'

'Humour?' asked Jacky. 'You're too kind to them, Pat. But do you think we could go on Daddy's yacht? It'd be a gorgeous trip,' she added wistfully.

'Just think—the South of France at this time of the year, the sunshine, the blue Mediterranean and—and everything.   Gosh, wouldn't it be wonderful?'

I was secretly touched by her enthusiasm.   When we had first met Jacky, she was too supercilious for words.   There was nothing that didn't bore her: or at any rate she managed to appear patronizing about every suggestion that was made.   But long since her sophisticated veneer had been stripped off and she was now a normal and cheerful young teen-ager like her two friends.   I began wondering whether there might be a plan we could work out—and what the snags might be—when the practical Jane broke into my thoughts.

'I'm with Jacky,' she said.   'This is far too good to miss.   How about our going there *on the yacht*?   That would cut out the problems of travelling overland.'

Jacky's face lit up as though someone had turned a switch.   'You're not always such a fool as you look,' she replied to Jane graciously.   Then a thought suddenly struck her.   She rustled over the pages of her father's letter.   'Oh dear,' she groaned, 'I knew he mentioned it somewhere.   Today's Wednesday, isn't it?   Daddy says he ordered the skipper to sail yesterday!'

'Seems odd,' murmured Jimmy.   'He must have known we would have to get there somehow.   It's quite a long walk if you turn right at Calais and just keep going.'

[5]

'What do you think, Pat?' was Jacky's appeal. 'You don't want us to miss this opportunity, do you? There must be some way we can get down there!'

'It's difficult,' I answered slowly. 'The cheapest way would be by train, I suppose, but it would take over a day, probably two days from here, and I honestly couldn't risk the three of you travelling all that way on your own. Some time or other I've got to go to Spain to see a horse I've been asked to buy and that's in the same general direction. But I can't get away for at least ten days because I've already promised to appear at various shows. Besides, the car must go in for an overhaul next week.'

'How about us flying?' asked Jacky. 'That's the quickest and simplest way.'

'Listen to Miss Midas,' Jane said. 'How about flying,' she mimicked. 'How about buying a Super Fortress and fitting it out with platinum propellers?'

'Jane's right, Jacky,' I said. 'Flying there would be terribly expensive.'

Their faces clouded over. Then Jimmy voiced the thoughts that must have been in all our minds. 'Your father's not an ass, Jacky,' he said. 'Unlike his daughter, of course. I can't think he would raise our hopes in this way unless he'd thought of an answer.'

Jane nodded. 'That makes sense,' she said. 'Come on, Jacky, read the letter again carefully. There may be a secret clue or something in it.'

'I doubt it,' Jacky replied dolefully. 'Daddy never has time to play games.'

The ever-observant Paddy, who had been watching the scene silently, broke in with, 'I don't want to be nosey, Jacky, but doesn't it say "P.T.O." at the bottom of the letter—just under your father's signature. He must have added a bit on the back.'

Jacky turned the last page over. 'So he has,' she said. 'Well done, Paddy.' She scanned the three or four lines of writing, then looked up with a puzzled expression. 'I don't get it,' she added. 'He says that he has thought of a means of transport—whatever that means means . . .'

'Rotten pun!' yelled the other two Jays in unison.

'. . . and I ought to be getting a communication with the details which he thinks Pat will agree to any time now.'

'No offence meant,' Jimmy commented, 'but your father uses pretty long-winded words, doesn't he? That must be the secret for getting on in business.'

Jane neglected the chance of pulling Jacky's leg further. 'I've got it,' she yelled. 'The other letter! You haven't read it yet, Jacky. That must be the answer. Quick, child, open it and see what it says!'

'Child yourself,' Jacky retorted and stuck out a pink tip of tongue. All the same, she wasted no time in ripping open the envelope and reading the contents. The rest of us waited in suspense.

When she looked up again after what seemed to be an age, she frowned but I thought I detected a sly gleam in her eyes. She said slowly, 'It's from my cousin Darcy.'

'Darcy?' echoed the other two Jays.

'Yes, Darcy de Vere. He's a cousin on my mother's side. She was a de Vere before she got married. That's why I have the name.'

'Darcy de Vere,' repeated Jane. 'I just don't believe it. No one could have a name like that.'

'Well, he has,' Jacky retorted sharply.

'Blow his name,' was Jimmy's comment. 'He can call himself Napoleon Bonaparte for all I care. What I want to know is—*what does he say?*'

'Oh, the letter,' Jacky answered languidly. 'I'll read it to you—it's quite short.' Taking a deep breath, she went on,

'My dear cousin,

Your esteemed parent has prompted me to present myself at the honoured establishment of Miserden to discuss matters of grave importance with your hostess, Miss Patricia Smythe, I understand her name to be. I have accordingly acquired that new-fangled means of transport, a motor vehicle, and propose to reach your vicinity, D.V., in the near future. Until then, I have the honour to be,

Your obedient servant and cousin,

Darcy.'

[8]

There was a deathly silence, broken by the crackling noise of Jacky's folding the letter in two and stuffing it defiantly back into the envelope. Then Jimmy let out a long whistle. 'Darcy de Vere,' he said slowly, rolling out each syllable. 'Are you sure his name isn't Charlie?'

Jane took the cue. 'Whatever his name, he sounds a proper charlie.'

I thought Jacky would spring to the defence of her cousin but she said meekly, 'Oh, Darcy's quite a decent fellow. He spends most of his time in the British Museum studying old books, so he can't help it if his writing's a bit old-fashioned. It's not really his fault that he thinks games like rugger and football are too rough for him. You see, it's those thick glasses he has to wear—like the bottoms of lemonade bottles. He's too short-sighted to play games. Besides, his beard would get in the way.'

We listened in fascinated horror to Jacky's description of her cousin. Then Jimmy turned to me and said, 'Could you make out what the letter meant, Pat? All that stuff about "D.V." or whatever it was. What was he trying to say?'

'It's the initials of two Latin words, Jim. It means "God willing".'

'I don't want to be blasphemous but . . .'

'Jimmy,' I said sharply.

'. . . Well, you know what I mean, Pat. Jacky's

bad enough but her precious cousin sounds the end.
A regular square, I'd say.'

'A proper creep,' added his sister, who spent much
of her spare time watching American films on
television.

'What's he coming here for—if that's what he
meant to say in the letter?' asked Jimmy. 'And
what's your father's idea, Jacky?'

'I reckon Daddy wants Darcy to escort us down
to the South of France,' she replied. 'Darcy's a
wizard at looking at museums and old buildings.
There must be a lot of them between here and there,
aren't there, Pat?'

'There certainly are,' I said.

'Well, there you are then,' she added triumphantly. 'Daddy probably guesses none of us did too
well at history last term and so he's arranged for
Darcy to take us on a conducted tour in France. It
wouldn't take much more than a fortnight if we
looked at several castles and things every day and
we ought to reach the South in time to spend at
least one day with Daddy.'

At that moment the other two Jays could have
posed for one of those Academy paintings entitled
'Gloom and Despair'. Their idea of a holiday in
France—or anywhere else for that matter—was
riding and swimming and perhaps some sailing,
with plenty of hot sunshine for them to sunbathe in
when they were momentarily resting from their

sports. Being lugged around musty old buildings and looking at paintings and statues was a penance to them, not a pleasure. The odd thing was that Jacky would normally be a hundred per cent on the same side but here she was, announcing the programme with relish. Perhaps she was being loyal to her cousin Darcy, the bookworm. I didn't want to pre-judge him at this stage but Jimmy's and Jane's descriptions seemed accurate enough.

'How old would your cousin be?' I asked Jacky.

'Oh, middle-aged, I think,' she replied airily. 'Of course, his beard makes him look a lot older. And he stoops rather—from bending over all those books. You've got to humour him a bit, because he doesn't like children—as he calls people our age—very much. Luckily, he's a bit deaf in one ear, so if you keep on the right side of him, you don't always have to whisper.'

Inwardly I groaned. Darcy de Vere seemed to live up to his name. Mr. Field, Jacky's father, was a very sensible man and I couldn't imagine that he would expect the Three Jays to spend a holiday traipsing in and out of museums and 'buildings of historical importance'. Particularly with a guide who used ponderously long words and must be an out-and-out bookworm. Perhaps it was all a mistake. It could be, I hoped wildly, that Darcy was merely going to do some research in the South of France and Mr. Field just wanted him to escort the Jays

[11]

there without stopping on the way to inspect the châteaux of the Loire or other historical places. But it didn't sound likely.

Jimmy pushed his empty plate away. 'I've lost my appetite,' he announced. 'It sounded so wonderful, too, when Jacky first told us. Just think of it—a holiday on the yacht in the South of France. And now this creep has to crop up. I only hope his "motor vehicle" breaks down!'

At that moment there was a noise outside the front door of Miserden House, a noise so loud that it penetrated even the centuries-old, thick stone walls to the back of the house and our dining room. I can only describe it as though some giant had ripped in half an enormous sheet of calico. It was followed by a second noise—a deep, drumming sound which died away into silence that you could almost touch. For a second we all seemed to freeze, looking at each other's startled faces. Then Jacky said quietly, 'I think that must be Darcy now.'

Without a word we pushed back our chairs. The Three Jays rushed ahead, while Paddy and I followed more sedately. Even so, we were eager to get our first glimpse of the classical scholar and his 'motor vehicle'.

We reached the now open front door, then stopped dead in our tracks. Drawn up ahead of us and almost blocking out the view across the Gloucestershire hills was an enormous green car. It had a

bonnet that seemed to stretch on indefinitely but finally ended in a high copper prow that gleamed in the morning sun. The bonnet was fastened down with two broad straps. There was no roof or hood but just a low, slanting windshield. The narrow wings reared proudly over the front wheels, then swept back to a running board; the handbrake was a massive affair fixed to the *outside* of the car. I did not need to glance at the winged 'B' on that handsome radiator to recognize the make. It was one of those rare masterpieces, a Le Mans type Bentley, a classic among motor cars nearly thirty years old and still, judging by the noise we had just heard, going strong.

And lolling back in the driver's seat was another strange specimen. Where were the long beard and the thick, pebble glasses that Jacky had described so vividly? Instead we gazed in silence at a lanky figure in a flying helmet with flaps undone and goggles pushed up on his forehead. Dancing blue eyes looked out on us from above a freckled face and a huge red handlebar moustache with the ends twirled arrogantly upwards. A spotted handkerchief round the neck and a rumpled tweed suit completed the ensemble and, as the figure vaulted lightly out of the seat on to the ground in front of us, I caught a glimpse of suède chukka boots. The figure waved a gloved hand and said, 'Wotcher, Jacky.'

Jimmy and Jane stood speechless with awe at this apparition. Gathering my own confused thoughts, I said, 'You'd better introduce us, Jacky.'

She turned obediently and said, 'May I present my cousin, Flight Lieutenant Darcy de Vere of the High Speed Experimental Squadron—Miss Pat Smythe, Miss Paddy Bury, her secretary and two of my so-called friends Jimmy and Jane who have just crept out from under a large stone.'

We shook hands in turn, mumbling 'How d'you do' in the English manner. Then the other two Jays turned to Jacky and hissed in unison, 'Beast!'

Darcy, as we were soon to call him, looked startled, so I hurried in with an explanation. 'I'm afraid my cousins weren't quite thinking you'd turn out like this. Jacky had led us to expect someone rather different.'

'She said you had a long beard and glasses,' said Jimmy. 'A classical scholar always reading old books,' he added bitterly.

'Dash it all, Jacky,' Darcy said, 'that's slander, I reckon. Me a classical scholar? The main reason I took up flying was because irregular verbs foxed me.'

There was already a look of hero-worship on Jimmy's eager face. 'What's the High Speed Squadron?' he asked. 'And what kind of planes do you fly?'

'Nothing but jets these days,' Darcy replied.

[15]

'You know, things that go wa-ah-ah-ah-ah—ooh!'
He swung one freckled hand past his face and gave
a realistic imitation of a plane breaking the sound
barrier.

'Jimmy,' I said, 'don't plague Mr.—Flight Lieutenant de Vere with all those questions now. There'll
be plenty of time later, I'm sure. Won't you come
in and have some coffee? We've only just finished
breakfast but we can easily get some more for you,
if you haven't had yours. You must have left
hours ago.'

'Thank you very much, ma'am,' said Darcy. 'I
could use a cup of coffee but no breakfast, thank you.
I had mine before I left London just an hour and
three-quarters ago.' He glanced at his wrist-watch
as he said it.

'An hour and three-quarters,' Jimmy echoed. 'But
we're a hundred miles from London here. That's
an average of—of—what's it an average of, Pat?'

I thought quickly. 'Nearly sixty miles an hour.'

'Sixty miles an hour!' said Jimmy with a whistle.
'Boy, that's travelling!'

Darcy grinned. 'Dash it all,' he said. 'Old
Bertha's no slowcoach, are you, sweetheart?' and
he gave an affectionate pat to the tall bonnet.

'What do you call it—her, I mean?' Jane asked.

'Bertha. Or sometimes Big Bertha. In the
First War the Germans had a huge gun they called
Big Bertha. She's not small and when she's in the

mood she'll go like a gun. Bertha the Bentley—it sounds right, don't you think?' He must have been about twenty-five but the eager way he spoke about his 'sweetheart' and his lack of pose made him seem for a moment a contemporary of the Three Jays.

We all trooped into the house in a procession. The walls of the corridor leading into the main hall are hung with plaques from the countless horse shows I have attended over the past ten years or so. Jane, who missed very little, spotted that Darcy wrinkled up his handlebar moustache and seemed to shy away as he walked past the plaques. When we finally sat down in the lounge and Paddy bustled off to get some fresh coffee made, Jane said to Darcy, 'You don't seem very fond of horses?'

Darcy shuddered. 'Dash it all,' he replied, 'if there's one thing I'm allergic to, it's that so-called four-legged friend. Horses—ugh!' and he gave a snort which was not unlike the noise one of the creatures he so disliked might have made.

'You don't like horses?' asked Jimmy in an incredulous and rather disappointed tone. 'We're all crazy about them here.'

'Well, each to his taste, I say,' Darcy remarked. 'Some people make pals with poisonous snakes. Others go in for tiger taming. There's no law that says you mustn't love a horse, I suppose. Personally, the only kind I can stand are the ones locked away under Bertha's bonnet!'

[17]

The Jays roared with laughter. Apart from Darcy's comical tone, they just couldn't believe that anyone existed without a passionate feeling for horses. Darcy had the passionate feeling right enough, it seemed, but it was directed the wrong way.

This was a puzzle worth probing, so I enquired, 'Why don't you like horses? I ought to warn you, perhaps, that you've landed among a crowd of enthusiasts here.'

He shuddered again. 'Nasty brutes,' he answered with distaste. 'If you stand too close behind them, they kick you and if you approach them from the front, they bite. Either way you can't win. Besides, I climbed aboard one once. I was so high off the ground sitting up there, I went rigid with fright, I can tell you. I came down in no mean hurry. Of course, the horse helped me down by giving a buck at the right moment, bless his treacherous little heart! Mind you, I made a perfect three-point landing— on one nose and two knees!'

The Three Jays burst out laughing again and I had to join them. Darcy, who flew jets at high altitudes, being scared of sitting on a horse four feet in the air. It seemed a wonderful joke.

Paddy arrived with the coffee and we sat around, drinking it. The ice had been shattered in a million pieces and I think we all felt we had known Darcy for ages and not for ten minutes or so. Suddenly there came an 'Ouch!' from Jacky and out of the corner of my eye I saw Jane give her a wicked jab.

'What's that for?' asked Jacky plaintively.

'That's for pulling our legs,' said Jane. 'A classical scholar, indeed! Thick glasses and a beard!'

Darcy smiled at this outburst. 'From the way Jacky described you,' I said, 'we were expecting a pompous middle-aged creature who always had his nose stuck in a book. Mind you, the letter you wrote—which Jacky read out to us—sounded that way.'

Darcy grinned. 'Oh, that's an old family joke,' he said. 'We always write long-winded letters to one another. I sat up half the night looking up words in the dictionary for that one.'

'Anyway,' Jacky argued, 'they made fun of your name. They said it sounded cissy. One of them— I won't say who—called you a proper charlie. How square can you be, Jimmy?' she asked innocently.

The other two Jays had the grace to blush but Darcy helped them out by saying, 'Well, dash it all, it is a bit of a silly name—although you can hardly blame me for it. My poor mum never realized what she was letting me in for when she got the parson to launch me with a name like that!'

There was a short silence which Jacky broke by exclaiming, 'I've got an idea!'

Jimmy and Jane groaned. They had had many a taste before of Jacky's 'ideas'.

Nothing daunted, Jacky plunged on, 'I vote we

re-christen you, Darcy, here and now. From this day forward I dub thee "Dashitall Darcy"—or "Dashitall" for short. How's that?'

Darcy gave a wide grin that made the tips of his enormous moustache quiver. 'Whatever you say, ma'am,' he drawled. 'I've been called worse things in the Air Force! Mind you, I can't think why you should pick out that particular nickname. Dash it all, it isn't as if I said "Dash it all" very often!'

So Dashitall he became and the nickname stuck to him ever afterwards.

By this time we had finished our coffee. Darcy glanced at his watch and said, 'We'd better get down to brass tacks, I guess. I've got to report back for duty this afternoon. And you kids will no doubt want to dash off and exercise your loathsome horses!'

'You'll be able to stay for lunch, won't you?' I asked.

'Love to, if you don't mind it being on the early side, ma'am.'

'And do please call me Pat. The other thing makes me feel too much like Royalty.'

'Thank you, ma'am—I mean, Pat.' He paused, then fumbled in a side pocket and took out a meer-schaum pipe, one of those huge, curly ones that looks like a fugitive from a brass band competition. He glanced at me for permission to go ahead and I nodded. Then, as he stuffed it with an enormous quantity of tobacco, lit it and blew out clouds of smoke, Dashitall Darcy said between puffs, 'This is the plot, as I see it. We need some careful co-ordination because it's a case of individual sorties, so to speak. Jacky's old man has ordered the yacht to sail to Cannes. I rang the skipper before he left yesterday and he reckons it'll take them ten days if they don't rush it. That means they'll arrive nine days from now—next Friday week, in fact. Now I've got to spend a few days at Marseilles on liaison duty with the French Air Force down there. It's up to me when I go and I think I can wangle some leave when I've done it. Normally I'd fly, of course, but I could arrange to drive there with Bertha. I'd like to try out her paces on those long, straight French roads—r-r-r-r-r-umph!' He imitated the snarling sound of the exhaust as he gripped an imaginary steering wheel in his hands. Then he went on, 'Jacky's father tells me in the letter that he'll be in New York until next Wednesday, today week, and then he'll fly to Nice, getting there on Friday, just about the time the yacht arrives at Cannes a few miles away. No problem there. Now, if you approve, Pat, I'll take the three of these'—he indicated the Jays—'down to Marseilles in Bertha, starting at the crack of dawn on Monday. I reckon we could do it in a couple of days if we push it a bit. Then I'll do my three days' liaison with the Frenchies and then we can all drive along the coast to have a holiday on the yacht. How about that?'

I thought for a moment. 'That's fine as far as it goes—but it doesn't go very far, I'm afraid. There are lots of snags. First, passports. None of the Jays has one and you can't get out of the country without it.'

'That's easy,' replied Dashitall Darcy. 'They could travel on mine. Or we could fix up passports for them in a couple of days. I've got a pal in the Foreign Office who'll pull some strings. Next objection?'

'I'm sure you'd look after them properly and not drive too fast through France . . .'

'Sure,' he grinned.

'. . . but what happens to them when you reach Marseilles? You'll be attached to the French Air Force but they can't live in barracks, or whatever it is, with you, can they? And I couldn't have them wandering around Marseilles on their own. It's a pretty tough place in spots, like any other big port.'

Darcy made a grimace. 'I forgot to lower my undercarriage when I landed on that one! You've got a point there, Pat. What on earth do we do with them while I'm on duty in Marseilles?'

'Couldn't you take us to Nice first and leave us on the yacht before you go on to wherever it is?' asked Jimmy.

'Ass!' said the two girls in chorus. 'The yacht won't get there till the end of the week,' added Jane.

There was a moment of gloomy silence. It had seemed such a wonderful plan for a holiday but none of us could see a way round this latest problem. Dashitall gazed at the moulded plaster ceiling as though he might pluck inspiration out of the air, while the Three Jays stared miserably at the floor. Then the germ of a thought flashed into my mind. I spent a few seconds in a feverish mental calculation, then said, 'I think I've got one of Jacky's wonderful ideas coming on.'

'What is it?' came the eager question from Jane.

'Yes, Pat—out with it!' Jimmy exclaimed.

'You've heard me talk about the Camargue? It's that area of flat, rather marshy land west of Marseilles where the River Rhône forks into two before it runs down to the sea. I'm sure I've told you about the Gardians of the marshes who are amazing horsemen.'

Jimmy and Jane nodded. Jacky asked, 'Wasn't there a film made about it? I saw it in London ages ago. All about the herds of wild horses that roam around.'

'That's right, Jacky,' I answered. 'It was called *Crin Blanc*. It's a French film.'

'I know,' said Jane. 'There's a picture from it at the very back of your *Book of Horses*.'

c   [23]

I smiled in appreciation. 'You've got a good memory, Janey,' I said.

Dashitall looked even gloomier. 'I knew it wouldn't be long before we got back to *that* subject,' he muttered. 'Anyway, Pat, after the geography lesson, what now?'

'This,' I said. 'I've got some good friends who live in the Camargue, not far from the ancient city of Arles. There's no reason why they shouldn't put the Three Jays up for a few days while you're in Marseilles. It would hardly be ten miles out of your way to drop the Jays off and you could collect them again after your spell of duty. In fact, I don't see why I shouldn't come down to the Camargue myself for a short holiday and then go on to Spain to see the horse I might buy. Could we work it in, Paddy?' I asked.

Paddy, who had been sitting silently up to this point, thought for a moment, then replied slowly, 'I think you could, Pat. You're jumping this Friday and Saturday and I'd half arranged for you to spend a couple of days in London at the beginning of next week but there's no great urgency for that trip. Mind you, you must be back by today fortnight because there's a big show on then.'

'That's all right, Paddy. I could fly down to the Camargue on Tuesday, spend three days there, cross into Spain at the week-end, look at the horse and fly back the following Monday or Tuesday. Yes, it'll work out just nicely.'

'You couldn't drive down with us, I suppose?' asked Jacky.

'Afraid not. I can't afford the time and, besides, there wouldn't be room in the car. Anyway, I doubt if my nerves would stand seven hundred miles in a monster like that! No offence meant,' I added hastily as I saw Darcy's moustache beginning to bristle at the implied insult. 'But perhaps you could pick me up at Marseilles Airport and we'll drive the last bit to the Camargue together.'

By this time the Three Jays were beaming. From the look on his face Jimmy was working up to an atrocious pun and, sure enough, out it came. 'I just knew everything was going to be Arles right,' he drawled in a would-be American accent. There was a flurry of blows as the other two set on him.

'Steady!' I yelled. 'You're not there yet. We've got heaps to do before you can even start. Passports, clothes to be sorted out and packed, lots of things.'

Not to be outdone by her brother, Jane chanted, 'I feel like singing' and before anyone could stop her, she began to the tune of 'A Bicycle Made for Two':

"'Darcy, Darcy, take me to Arles with you,
Darcy, Darcy, we'll find a horse for you!
It's only an ancient Bentley,
So you'll have to drive it gently.

[25]

Your streamlined whiskers
Will . . ."

Oh dear, I can't think of a rhyme for whiskers,' she ended lamely.

'Just as well,' commented the subject of her song grimly but the twinkle in his eye gave him away.

'So that's more or less arranged,' I said. 'Oh, one thing—and a very important thing, too. We're talking glibly about your flying the car over next Monday but I happen to know that the Silver City flights from Lydd to Le Touquet are just about booked out at this time of the year. And it's not as though you were trying to squeeze a baby car on board the plane. Bertha must be over sixteen feet long, isn't she, Dashitall?'

He nodded and Jane, always anxious to emulate Jimmy when it came to a pun, added, 'Quite a problem—finding a berth for Bertha!' The other two Jays wrinkled their noses in scorn and the rest of us shuddered.

'We'll get round it all right, Pat,' said Darcy. 'They're good chaps, those Silver City people. Besides, one of their senior men on the flight bookings side used to be my squadron leader before he left the R.A.F. If I could use your phone, please, I'll start giving the right strings a gentle tug here and now.'

'Yes, please do,' I answered. 'In fact, we'd better all start organizing things. Spain's about the only

European country that insists on visas and, as you're not going there this trip, you won't need them on top of your passports. But we've got plenty else to think about and get ready in the next three or four days. While Darcy's ringing up his friends and Paddy and I are sorting out other matters, you Three Jays had better keep out of our way. I know, you can go and exercise the ponies up in the paddock. It won't hurt them to get a good deal of work between now and the week-end, since they'll have a pretty lazy time while you're away. Would you like the Jays to show you round the stables, Darcy?' I added jokingly.

His jaw dropped. 'Dash it all,' he said, 'I'd rather go ten rounds in a cage with a man-eating tiger! Horses—ugh!'

Everyone burst out laughing and then the party broke up. The rest of the morning passed in a flash and, when we assembled for an early lunch, there was some excellent progress to report. Darcy had fixed the cross-Channel plane flight for nine o'clock next Monday morning, which would mean leaving Miserden at the unearthly hour of five. He would spend Sunday night with us beforehand. Paddy in her turn had booked my flight to Marseilles for the Wednesday morning and I had written a note to my friends in the Camargue, telling them of the plan and asking if they would be kind enough to look after the Three Jays while Darcy was in Marseilles and

[27]

give them plenty of riding. My friends had had a large family of their own, now grown up, and I knew that they adored having young people around them. The whole family had learned to ride almost before they walked and I was sure that the Three Jays would slip happily into the horsey atmosphere.

As Darcy would not be able to return to England on the yacht, since he would have to drive Bertha back, we decided it was no use letting the Jays travel on his passport. This meant rushing them into Cheltenham for passport photographs to be taken and developed immediately. Jimmy took one look at the result and said, 'Blimey, Son of Dracula walks again!' It was not a bad summing-up, either! Paddy, without whose memory and methodical ways Miserden House would come to a grinding halt in no time at all, managed to dig out some spare passport application forms from one of her files. We got the Jays to fill them in and sign them, so that Darcy could take them back to London with him.

And so, shortly after lunch, he leaped into Bertha's cockpit—as he called it. The engine roared and spat blue smoke out of its monstrous exhaust. The back tyres spun in a shower of gravel and the big green car lurched up the hill, gathering speed in a crescendo of ear-splitting noise. Darcy waved a gloved hand and we caught a last glimpse of his ginger moustache, the tips flattened by the air-pressure above the low windshield, as he turned to give us the 'thumbs-up' sign before he disappeared.

We were all so busy getting ready for the Jays' big adventure that Darcy had hardly gone before it seemed that he was back again on the Sunday afternoon. By then we were all set, with only last-minute items to be shoved into already bulging suitcases. There had been the usual good-hearted rows and bickering, of course. Jacky had never learned the meaning of the phrase 'travelling light' and she produced four or five enormous cases, each one larger than the last, in expensive pigskin with her initials in gilt on the sides. She solemnly began to pack the whole of her extensive wardrobe into them and, as Jimmy remarked maliciously, anyone would have thought she was joining the Trans-Antarctic Expedition to judge by the different items she thought were essential. I managed to persuade her that this was to be a summer holiday and not a Command Performance. My friends in the Camargue, I said, would not feel insulted if she left her three different sets of riding clothes at home and merely packed, or rather travelled in, her old jeans and tweed coat.

At last Monday morning dawned, although we had beaten it by a long head. The household was up at four, yawning and rubbing sleep out of heavy eyes, as we bolted a quick breakfast and lugged the suitcases out to the waiting car. The front of the house

was still deep in shadow when the Three Jays
scrambled into the open Bentley. To save argument,
they had agreed to take it in turns to sit in the front
with Darcy. Jimmy, as the oldest, was the first to
have the privileged position but the two girls, ardent
feminists when it came to matters like this, muttered
under their breaths, 'Boys first, of course!'

The time had come. 'Got everything?' I asked.
'Specially passports?'

Darcy nodded in the pale morning light and tapped
his breast pocket reassuringly.

'You will take good care of them, won't you?' I
went on. 'And, please, Dashitall—not too fast on
those French roads!'

He patted my shoulder as though I were a little
girl. 'Not to worry, Pat,' he replied. 'Dash it all,
I'll treat them as though I were carrying a cargo of
eggs in the back. You know, "Fragile—this side up"
kind of thing.'

'Well, as long as you don't crack one of them!' I
retorted.

Darcy jumped into the driver's seat and started the
engine. The noise set a dog barking on a farm a
mile away.

'Goodbye—and have a wonderful time!' Paddy
and I yelled over the din as Darcy revved up.

The Jays waved and Jacky shouted, 'See you in
Marseilles—whoopee!' Then they were gone to a
snarling roar of the engine.

Paddy and I walked slowly back into the house which suddenly seemed empty without the Three Jays. 'I hope they'll be all right,' she said.

'I'm sure they will. Darcy's very reliable underneath it all. But I bet they'll have an adventure or two before they reach Arles!'

I was a better prophet than I knew at the time.

CHAPTER 2

Southward Bound!

The next time I saw my young friends was several days and seven hundred miles away. And so I have had to piece together their experiences in getting to Marseilles from the individual accounts they gave me later. This part of the story is therefore 'hearsay', as the lawyers call any evidence in which the witness was not actually present at the time. I think, however, that you will find it more or less accurate. I say 'more or less' because, although the Three Jays always tell the truth when it matters, they also have the knack of slightly improving on the facts!

*　　　*　　　*

DARCY swung the big Bentley south towards Swindon, aiming to hit the main A4 road at Hungerford. His plan was to circle round London and avoid being held up in traffic jams by going via Newbury, Basingstoke, Farnham and Guildford, then follow the A25 road towards Tonbridge. The open car rushed ahead through the country lanes while the sun, still low on the horizon, striped the road with flickering shadows and pushed back the early morning mist from the quiet fields.

The wind of their movement swirled into the back

seats and Jane and Jacky snuggled gratefully down under the travelling rug they had wrapped round themselves. The hum of the tyres and the sight of the hedges rushing rearwards seemed to have a hypnotic effect on them and after a while they began to doze. It was still an hour or so before their normal getting-up time and they had not fully recovered from the excitement of actually starting on the long journey, the first time either of them had left England.

Jimmy, however, was on the alert in the bucket seat alongside Darcy in front. He ducked low to keep out of the rushing wind but his eyes drank in the wonderful collection of knobs and dials on the dashboard. Darcy had pointed out the rev counter and the speedometer and Jimmy watched the swinging needles with rapt attention. From time to time he was fascinated to see the technique for pulling the huge car around a bend. He noticed how Darcy sat relaxed and yet instantly on the alert, his gloved hands lightly moving on the cord-bound steering wheel. As they roared towards a corner, he saw that Darcy stabbed at the clutch with his left foot, flicked the gear lever into neutral with his left hand, paused fractionally while he gunned the accelerator with his right foot, then slammed home the lever into the lower gear a split second before he lifted his left foot again and the engine whined harshly in response.

Round they would go and the hedges skated past Jimmy's eyes in a mad blur as the car described its curve, then straightened out and continued its swift progress along the empty road.

After a while Jimmy's eyelids began to droop. His chin settled by degrees on to his chest and he slipped lower down in the bucket seat. He, too, was beginning to feel the effects of the tension and the mounting suspense during the past few days. His head nodded and though he jerked himself fiercely to attention, the effort was too great. Before long he was sleeping as soundly as the two rear passengers. Darcy glanced down and smiled at the peaceful sight alongside him.

There was little traffic at this hour of the morning and they made good progress. By half past six the car was only a few miles outside Farnham and, although it was held up for several minutes in the twisty, narrow side-streets of Guildford—where the stops and starts roused the Three Jays from their slumbers—it was racing along the broad highway under the lea of the chalk hills towards Dorking when they were still rubbing their eyes and sitting up to take notice.

'France looks remarkably like England, doesn't it?' Jacky asked Jane conversationally.

Jane looked around her. 'We're not there yet, stupid!' she exclaimed. 'We're *still* in England. Look, we're on the left side of the road. In France they drive on the right.'

'You don't say?' said Jacky. 'Where did you pick

up all that culture? Anyway, judging from the way Dashitall drives, you can't always tell which side of the road you're meant to be on!'

The object of this slander overheard her above the roar of the wind and turned to grin, then swung round hurriedly to avoid an early morning milk cart that was ambling along the road ahead.

'Careful!' Jacky yelled. 'We like milk for breakfast but preferably not whisked up too much! Talking of breakfast,' she went on, 'I dreamt we were already in France and tucking into a marvellous meal. Turkey and ham and some hot sizzling sausages and ice cream and hot rolls and—and . . .'

'Stop torturing me,' Jane cut in. 'It's ages since we ate anything and, besides, I was too excited to taste that snack we had before we left Miserden. Any chance of stopping for a second breakfast?' she said in Darcy's ear as she leaned forward and nudged him.

'I'd rather get on with the journey,' he replied. 'We've still got about seventy miles to go and there's always a hold-up at the bottleneck in Tonbridge. We can have some coffee and a snack at the airport restaurant. Here's something to be getting on with.' He dug a hand in his pocket and pulled out a big bar of chocolate which he held up. 'Any offers?' he asked.

There was a wild scramble as the Three Jays swooped, a rustle of silver paper and then a steady munching noise.

'Anyone ever call you the Three Vultures?' queried Darcy mildly, but their mouths were fully occupied with the chocolate which prevented a quick reply.

By a quarter past eight they were well clear of Tonbridge and into the flat area of the Romney Marshes with their winding dyke-lined roads and level green fields that stretched away to the horizon on either side. Bertha sped through villages that were a cluster of tiny cottages with a noble stone church standing aloof perhaps a hundred yards away, its spire soaring above the elm-trees around it. At last, when they could see the dim outline of New Romney in the distance, they came to a road junction with a signpost pointing to Lydd and 'Ferryfield', as the Silver City airport was called. Darcy swung the high bonnet sharply to the right and, minutes later, they were rolling up the approach road to the airport. There was a garage just outside the fence and Darcy pulled up to fill his tank. The red-faced attendant told him in the burring accent of the local Marshmen that he was only allowed to have the tank three-quarters full when boarding the plane. If the tank was full to overflowing and any petrol spilt during a bumpy flight, there might be a risk of fire. While Darcy was busy working out how many gallons he needed to get up to the three-quarters mark, Jane said to Jacky, 'Did he say something about a bumpy flight?'

Jacky knew that the other two had never been airborne before, whereas she held the proud record of having flown twice—from London to Liverpool and back—on a business trip with her father. 'Oh, yes,' she answered with all the airy assurance of a veteran. 'You've got to be prepared for a really rough time. On these cross-channel flights, it can be terribly bumpy.' She dredged into her imagination and came up with, 'Why, I believe on one flight it was so bad that someone who took a bottle of milk with them found it had turned to butter when they landed— with all the shaking!'

Jane's face dropped but Darcy, who had overheard the last remarks, broke in. 'Nuts to you, dear cousin,' he said. 'Don't you listen to her, Janey. These flights across the Channel are as smooth as silk. Dash it all, you're only airborne for about twenty minutes—and they provide strong brown paper bags for characters like Jacky here!'

He could almost feel the heat of Jacky's glare on the back of his neck as he paid the garage attendant, then drove the Bentley the short distance to the airport car park. There were already a few cars lined up and Darcy stopped alongside them. 'There we are,' he said. 'First stage completed according to plan. Bring your hand luggage and we'll go and chase that second breakfast. We've got just ten minutes in hand before they call us forward to go through the Customs and board the plane.'

'What about Bertha?' Jimmy asked. 'Don't you have to drive her aboard?'

'Heavens, no,' Darcy replied. 'That's the beauty of going this way. I leave the ignition key in and the next thing we'll see is Bertha going gently up the ramp into the aircraft. And on the other side the same thing happens in reverse. By the time we're out of the ship and past the Customs, Bertha will be waiting for us alongside the barrier.' Spotting the mystified expression on the girls' faces, he added, 'You see, they have expert drivers on the staff here and at Le Touquet whose job is to get the cars in and out of the planes. It takes a bit of practice to drive a car up the steep ramp fast enough so that it doesn't stall and stop half way up and yet not so fast that it doesn't charge right through the compartment for the cars and come out the other side!'

He led them through the modern hall of the main airport building where he stopped briefly to hand over his carnet to the authorities and collect landing cards which the Three Jays filled in while sipping coffee and munching biscuits at the counter just round the corner. Enormous windows stretched along the side of the building facing the runways. Jimmy was almost too fascinated in watching the huge, clumsy looking freight-planes lumbering up to the tarmac apron to do justice to his hunger. He sat in a chair by the windows, absent-mindedly eating while he watched one plane halt about twenty yards away. Two great jaws opened slowly in the front and an attendant wheeled a ramp up against the yawning cavity. Within a few moments a car drove slowly towards the foot of the ramp, climbed it with much revving of the engine and then disappeared inside. Two more small cars followed it in quick succession and, before Jimmy could swallow his mouthful of biscuit, the ramp was wheeled away, the wide jaws slowly came together and the plane was ready to take off.

'Marvellous, isn't it?' he sighed. 'I could spend the rest of the holiday sitting here and just watching them load the planes.'

Just then Darcy and the Three Jays heard their names called out on the loudspeaker. The impersonal crackling voice asked them to report at once to the rear of the building where they would be conducted through the Customs. It admonished them to have passports and landing cards ready.

'Press on,' Darcy commented. 'The pilot must have wound up that large rubber band! We're on our way.'

They were shepherded down a corridor in the wooden hut alongside the airport building, past a barrier where a bored-looking man glanced at their passports ('I have to make a frightful face to look like mine,' said Jacky. 'Nonsense,' replied Jane, 'just look natural—he'll recognize you at once!'), into another small hut where they waited perhaps two minutes and then out on to the tarmac apron and up a short flight of steps into the plane. They

D

discovered four or five rows of green leather armchairs in the passenger compartment and, through a half open door in the bulkhead in front of them, they could just catch a glimpse of Bertha securely lashed to the floor and the sides of the aircraft. There was a slight kefuffle as they sorted themselves out, fastened their safety belts and settled in their seats. There were only four other passengers on board, a middle-aged man and his wife and two young men with rucksacks and open-necked shirts. Jimmy had spotted a small, family saloon being driven into the plane after Bertha and two motor-scooters, so he was quite sure who owned which. (He was later rudely disappointed when at Le Touquet, the middle-aged, mild-looking couple mounted the scooters and went pop-pop-pop up the road and the two young men stowed their rucksacks into the small saloon before driving off.)

Soon the freight plane had rumbled to the far edge of the runway, revved each engine in turn, then waddled with increasing speed into the wind. While Darcy bought some duty-free cigarettes and whisky ('Purely medicinal, of course,' he muttered to Jacky alongside him) from the steward, Jimmy and Jane watched in fascination through the perspex window the lonely cottages tilting away underneath them as the aircraft lumbered into the air. Within minutes they saw its elongated shadow slide over a barren stretch of shingle off Dungeness Point and then the sea was far below, a pearly grey shot with green strands and the waves like wrinkles crawling towards the shore.

Darcy had hardly smoked the first of his duty-free cigarettes when the warning light—NO SMOKING FASTEN YOUR SEAT-BELTS—flashed on the bulkhead in front. Jimmy and Jane had prudently kept theirs fastened all the time but Jacky only just managed to root around and find the loose end of hers between the seats when the plane came in over low sand banks and dunes that might almost have been a continuation of the English coastline. It circled Le Touquet Airport, lost height in the circuit, then straightened out as it approached the runway. The earth which had seemed to move so slowly beneath them now came rushing past the windows. The plane appeared to drop suddenly, there was a slight jar as the wheels grazed the runway and then it settled and slowed, finally coming to a halt on a similar tarmac apron near an enormous hangar and in front of an airport building that was not unlike the one they had left only twenty minutes earlier. The aircraft doors were flung back, the steward said mechanically, 'Mind your heads, please,' and crouching through the low opening, they skipped down the steps on to the soil of France. In less than ten minutes they had gone through the Customs and bundled into the inviting seats of Bertha while an A.A. man grinned cheerfully at their excited faces and handed over the buff-coloured carnet to Darcy.

'Well, it's heigh-ho for the open road,' said Darcy, as he started the engine. 'Paris, here we come!'

A thought struck Jane. 'I suppose you know the way all right,' was the half-statement, half-query she made.

'Know the way?' he exclaimed. 'You might as well ask me if I know my own face!'

'Well, do you?' she persisted. 'Know the way, I mean.'

He thought for a moment. 'Well, sort of,' he admitted. 'You follow the road straight ahead until you come to Etaples. Then I think you take the first right over the bridge and follow your nose.' He pronounced the name of the town to rhyme with 'Naples'. 'Anyway,' he went on, 'if we get stuck, we can always ask our way.'

'I suppose you're good at French,' said Jane the inquisitor.

'Good? Dash it all, I know French like—like . . .'

'You know your own face,' they all chorused.

Darcy grinned a little sheepishly. He let in the clutch and Bertha roared away down the avenue lined with pine trees. There were signs in English telling them to keep to the right of the road. None of the Three Jays felt any different driving 'on the wrong side' until another car came along towards them. It seemed so odd to have traffic approaching you on the left hand.

Soon they came to a wide roundabout and Darcy slowed down. A gendarme was directing the traffic. As Bertha drew up, the Jays gazed at this strange phenomenon and noticed his lightish blue uniform, his black leather belt with a pistol holster stuck menacingly in it, his white gloves and lanyard and his round peaked cap. The gendarme had his whistle in his mouth and when he moved his arms to let another stream of traffic through, he gave a sharp toot on the whistle.

Darcy was taking no chances. He stopped alongside the gendarme and said, 'Bong joower—Paris?' pronouncing the last word in the English way.

The Frenchman looked at him pityingly and pointed silently to an enormous arrow that said, ETAPLES PARIS.

Darcy nodded his thanks. 'Mercy buckup,' he said, 'mercy very much. There,' he added as they drove off, 'what did I tell you? I'm an old hand at this French lark.'

Jacky turned round and stared at the other two who were now sitting in the back. Jane gave a slight shake of her head. They did not share Darcy's confidence in his own powers as a linguist.

Bertha went over a wide bridge, swung right down a cobbled side street and was soon in open country. The road was almost narrow enough to be called a lane and it twisted from side to side like a demented worm, as Jacky described it. Thick hedges on either side made it impossible for a driver to see far ahead. They soon caught up with a big, six-wheeler lorry with a kind of chimney stack on top belching smoke and followed it in single file at a sedate twenty miles an hour.

'I imagined the French roads were all straight and wide,' Jimmy commented. 'This one could almost be an English main road! At this rate, it'll take us weeks to get there.'

'Patience,' Darcy replied. 'This is only the early part. Once we're a bit inland, we can open her up.'

They passed through several villages on the road to Montreuil and noticed that, although the roads out in the open country were tarmac, nearly all the villages still had cobbled streets over which Bertha bounced and grumbled in her springs. The houses were built right up against the edge of the road, with no pavements and no small strip of garden in front, as there would have been in an English village. Most of the houses looked rather tumbledown with plaster peeling off the walls and the fact that they were almost uniformly painted in drab tones of buff and brown did not add to the general gaiety.

'Pretty poverty-stricken, aren't they?' Jane said.

'Don't you believe it,' Darcy told her. 'That pal of mine in the Foreign Office says that France is the richest country in Europe. These characters that look like hungry peasants have each got a big bag of gold underneath the mattress, he told me. They don't believe in paying taxes!'

Once the big Bentley had negotiated the steep, twisty streets into Montreuil (which none of the four passengers could pronounce properly), it reached the flat countryside of Northern France. Now the roads were straight and wide, lined with avenues of poplars as windbreaks. There was little traffic about, an occasional farm cart wandering on to the main road from the neighbouring fields or one of the popular makes of French car, a Renault or a Citröen. Darcy gave Bertha her head and she responded willingly, snarling down the road to Paris at a steady seventy-five miles an hour. Whenever she came up behind another car going in the same direction, Darcy would give a blast on the hooter before sweeping past.

'Why do you keep hooting at everything you pass?' asked Jacky from the front seat. 'Bit rude, isn't it?'

'Not a bit,' he replied. 'Just the opposite, in fact. In England, people drive quietly and it would be reckoned bad manners to give them a toot every time you overtake but on the Continent it's different. The driver in front expects you to warn him that you're coming up fast and are going to overtake, so that he can make room for you.'

'I can't say I've noticed anyone making room,' she

commented. 'Most of 'em either go faster or edge out towards the middle of the road, just to make it more difficult!'

'That's the French for you,' he smiled. 'It's that Gallic dash of theirs. You see that character there?' he asked, as he swung Bertha past an old Citröen with a cloth roof attached with press studs. A fat man was driving it and he glared and waggled his elbows to urge on his aged rattletrap as the Bentley came alongside, then raced ahead. 'He's not chugging along to market. He's driving for the honour of France!'

Jimmy leant forward from the back seat. 'Do you understand all these road signs we keep on passing, Dashitall?' he queried.

'Of course,' was the airy reply. 'Dash it all, haven't you kids realized yet that I'm an expert when it comes to Continental driving.'

'Well, what does that one mean that you see at the beginning of every village? It's a circle divided in two and in the top half there's a little picture of a lorry with the figure "40" underneath and in the bottom half a car with "60" underneath it.'

'Use your loaf,' said Darcy. 'All that means is that lorries mustn't exceed forty miles an hour through the village and cars mustn't exceed sixty.'

'That seems pretty fast,' Jane commented. 'Sixty miles an hour through a village is dangerous, I should think.'

'Well, we're doing fifty through this one,' Darcy retorted. 'Didn't I tell you just now that the French are fast drivers. They wouldn't stand for the kind of speed limits we have in England.'

They were clear of the village and out on the open road again when Jane said, 'Don't look round now but there's a motor-bike chasing us. It's shifting, too.'

'I'll give him shift,' Darcy said. 'Watch him disappear into the background,' he added and pressed his right foot harder against the accelerator.

But the grim-faced motor cyclist, who was dressed in a black leather jerkin with a black crash helmet on his head, stuck close behind. With his left hand he kept waving at Bertha's passengers and, not to be outdone, the Three Jays waved back.

'That's a queer hooter he's got,' Jimmy commented. 'It makes a kind of wailing noise—more like a siren.'

'Jolly unsporting,' Darcy said. 'Just because he's not quick enough to overtake, he needn't lose his temper and make all that row.'

They had reached a long straight stretch and the words were hardly out of Darcy's mouth when the impetuous motor cyclist disproved them by racing alongside. He shouted something unintelligible, then accelerated level with Bertha's offside front wheel and began to edge inwards.

'What's he up to?' Darcy exclaimed. 'He'll have

us in the ditch if he plays games like that. I'll give him a piece of my mind!'

'In your fluent French?' Jane slily enquired.

Darcy eased up and the motor cyclist shot ahead, then halted and swung his bike across their path so that Darcy had to stop dead. As he cleared his throat in readiness to do verbal battle with the man, the Three Jays spotted that the motor cyclist had a pistol strapped to his belt.

'Gosh, it's a hold-up,' breathed Jacky excitedly. She was an ardent fan of the 'Highway Patrol' series on television.

'It's a hold-up all right,' Jane said. 'But not the sort you're thinking of. I bet he's a speed cop—and he doesn't look too friendly either!'

By this time the man had leapt off his motor-bike which he propped up in Bertha's path to prevent their getting away. He strode over and glared down at Darcy, then burst into a flood of unintelligible French. 'I say,' muttered Darcy, 'this is too bad. How can you argue with a chap when you can't understand him?'

'Fox him with your fluent French,' suggested Jane.

Darcy took the hint and started off with his standby of 'Bong joower,' to which he added as an after-thought, 'monsewer'. The gendarme—for Jane had been right in her guess—brushed aside this response with an abrupt wave of his gloved fist

[49]

and then continued to shoot questions at them in French.

'He's saying something about *papiers*, I think,' Jimmy said. 'That means "papers" in English. He wants to see your papers.'

'Tell him we left England too early to buy a paper,' Darcy said.

'Not that kind of paper, silly,' cut in Jacky. 'He wants to see your documents—passports and things.'

'Well, dash it all, why doesn't he say so?' Darcy grumbled.

'He is saying so,' they chorused.

Darcy rummaged in the side pocket of the car and dug out a folder containing his passport, carnet, international driving licence and the green insurance papers. The speed cop flicked through them but didn't appear to understand them any more than Darcy understood him. Then he burst into another impassioned oration and with a gloved finger scrawled a diagram in the dusty corner of Bertha's windshield. He drew the roadsign they had recently discussed, with the picture of a car and a lorry and the figures '40' and '60'. Then he wrote the word 'KILOS' in block capitals backwards so that they could read it properly through the windscreen.

'What's he playing at?' Darcy demanded. 'Drawing pictures all over the place. I don't get it.'

Jane gave a jump. 'I do,' she said. 'The penny's dropped now. I ought to have thought of it sooner because we've just done the metric system in school. The French don't think in miles the way we do,' she explained to Darcy. 'They use kilometres which are something over a thousand yards long. To change them to miles, you have to multiply by five and divide by eight. That sign he's drawn doesn't mean the speed limit through the last village was sixty miles an hour—which seemed too fast anyway —but *sixty kilometres per hour.* That's three hundred divided by eight—help me, somebody—it's—it's a bit under forty miles an hour, isn't it?'

'No wonder he chased after us,' Jimmy said. 'You were doing over fifty through that last village.'

'How do we get out of this one, I wonder?' asked Darcy. 'It won't help our holiday if we all have to go to gaol for the next fortnight.'

'Maybe Devil's Island?' Jacky suggested. Her taste tended to run to the sensational.

The speed cop had fallen silent and was watching them suspiciously, obviously not understanding their chatter. Then Jane said, 'Let me have a go. It can't be worse than this deadlock.' She looked up at the speed cop and gave him an ingratiating smile. '*Pardonnez-lui,*' she went on slowly, indicating the crestfallen Darcy. '*Il est un peu fou et il ne sait pas les* —what's the French for "customs"?—ah, I remember —*les coutumes français.*' She paused, then stumbled on with, '*Je connais que maintenant il conduira l'auto tres tranquillement*—if there is such a word.'

'What's she saying?' asked Darcy suspiciously. 'It sounded a bit off to me.'

'She said you were nuts,' Jacky replied, 'and didn't really know what you were doing but with us looking after you things will be all right now.'

'Did she?' Darcy grunted. 'You just wait till we get rid of this tough-looking merchant.'

The speed cop looked from one to another with a bemused expression on his face. Then he thrust the folder back into Darcy's hands, wagged a forefinger at them, shrugged his shoulders in a typical Gallic way as if to say, 'Ah, these English!' and swaggered off to his bike. He kicked it into life and went screaming up the road while each of Bertha's occupants drew a deep breath.

'That was a nasty moment,' Jimmy commented. 'I thought we were for it then.'

Jacky added, 'We would have been if it weren't for our driver's fluent lack of French! Oh, Dashitall, I thought you were going to blind him with science and gabble back at him but all you did was sit there dumb.'

Darcy gave a rueful grin. 'Dash it all,' he said, 'that chap must have been speaking a dialect—that's why I couldn't follow him properly. If he had spoken with the kind of French accent I'm used to, I'd have seen him off smartly enough!'

'No one else speaks with "the kind of French accent" you're used to!' was Jacky's cheeky retort.

Jimmy and Jane began chanting quietly, 'Sixty miles an hour, sixty miles an hour!' Darcy gave up the lost battle, saw the funny side and laughed out loud, then let in the clutch and drove Bertha more sedately up the road towards Paris.

CHAPTER 3

Puncture, Politesse and Picasso

THE next three hours of their journey slid by uneventfully. They passed through Abbeville and Beauvais, the latter resplendent with shiny new buildings to replace the great damage it had suffered during the war from bombing and the German occupation. North of Paris they left Route One and skirted round the big city through St. Germain and Versailles. Darcy drove slowly across the great square in front of the historic chateau and they were tempted—'for culture's sake', as Jacky put it—to stop and walk through the famous gardens and inspect the state-rooms. But hunger and the urge to drive on south were too strong and they pressed on, turning off the ring road just before Orly Airport in the direction of Fontainebleau. They pulled up in the main square and Darcy took Jane, who had now been officially instated as interpreter, into a grocer's shop where they bought a bottle of red wine, some cheese, a large bunch of grapes, some pears and, next door, two long crusty French loaves. Once they were clear of the town, Darcy swung off the broad avenue through the Forest and stopped under the shade of the trees. The Three Jays leapt out, stretched their cramped limbs and then sat down again to devour the picnic lunch Darcy was spreading on the warm grass.

It was nearly two o'clock in the afternoon and the Three Jays had eaten nothing since the snack at Ferryfield. So they set to with even more than their usual gusto. For a while there was silence apart from the chattering of the birds in the tall trees that over-hung the avenue and the swishing of tyres when an occasional car rushed past. Darcy, a more sparing eater than the Jays, finished first. He picked up the bottle of red wine and then looked round enquiringly. 'I must say we're bright,' he said. 'Bought a bottle of the old *vino* and nothing to open it with.'

'Try Jimmy's penknife,' Jane suggested. 'It's got enough gadgets.'

Jimmy held a chunk of French loaf to his mouth with one hand while he dug in his pockets with the other, finally emerging with the famous penknife. His mouth was too full for him to speak, so he merely held out the knife for Darcy to take.

'Quite a weapon,' Darcy commented, looking in wonder at the various blades. 'You could just about decarbonize Bertha with this as a tool!' There was no corkscrew on it but he selected a marlin spike type of blade and began to dig out the cork. At last the job was done and the cork was partly in bits on the grass and partly shoved down to float on top of the wine.

'Seeing it was my knife that got it open, I suppose you'll give me my share,' asked Jimmy.

'Yes—and I helped you to buy it in the first place,' Jane added.

'After all, I'm your cousin,' Jacky cut in, 'and blood's thicker than water.'

'And wine, too,' Jane retorted.

'Here,' Darcy said, 'why don't the three of you drink it all and I'll just sit and watch you! Actually, I don't see why you shouldn't have a drop. French kids drink wine and it doesn't seem to hurt them. But take it easy. I don't want it to go to your head and have you behaving like a lot of drunken sailors! One brush with the police is enough for one day.'

They had brought two enamel mugs and Jacky unscrewed the top of the vacuum flask to make a third. Darcy was resigned to drinking out of the bottle, which he proceeded to do with a lusty swig after he had poured about half a cupful into each of their containers. The Three Jays sipped their wine more gingerly, noticing the slightly sour metallic taste and the warm glow it left in their stomachs.

'Is this vintage wine?' Jacky asked, a little anxious to show that she knew the right terms.

Darcy looked dubiously at the bottle. 'If this is vintage stuff, I'm a monkey's uncle. . . .'

'Go on, Jacky,' Jane urged, 'call him uncle!'

'. . . As I was saying when I was rudely interrupted,' Darcy went on with a grin, 'I reckon this is what they call *vin ordinaire*. It only cost two hundred and fifty francs, a bit under four bob, and you wouldn't get the real McCoy at that price. Anyway, it goes down the right way, so who's worrying?'

Having said which, he settled himself full length on the grass, tipped his cap over his eyes (the flying helmet had been left behind in England so as not to 'frighten the natives', as he put it) and proceeded to doze off in the sunshine. The Three Jays were too excited to follow his example and they chatted quietly, discussing the Forest of Fontainebleau and imagining how the Kings of France had ridden through it hunting stags. From hunting they quickly got on to their favourite topic of ponies and wondered, a shade wistfully, how Pickles, Jacky's property, and the other two ponies were faring in their absence. Then they looked ahead a day and a half to the moment when they would arrive in the Camargue and find fresh ponies to ride. The thought made them eager to press on with the journey and Jacky said, 'Just look at Dashitall snoring away peacefully there. At this rate we'll never reach the home of Pat's friends. I vote we give him a nudge and wake him up!'

This they promptly did and Darcy sat up, grunting and blinking. 'Bloomin' slave-drivers,' he muttered. 'Can't give a chap a moment's peace, can you? I've driven you over three hundred miles today, I'd have you know. What's the hurry, anyway?'

'We'd like to press on,' Jacky answered mildly. 'We're anxious to do some riding in the Camargue.'

Darcy shuddered. 'I might have guessed it,' he said. 'That's all you think about—riding, horses, stables—horrible creatures that prance all over the place and bite you if you aren't careful.'

'Who?—us or the horses?' Jane asked.

'Anyway, they don't break speed limits through villages,' Jacky observed.

Darcy laughed. 'All right, you win. I'll never hear the last of that episode. Come on, then, don't hold me back.' He jumped to his feet and began to pack up the left-overs from lunch. The Jays did their share and then climbed into the car, switching round so that Jane now had the front passenger seat. Before he started the engine, Darcy took out a folding map and began to study it. 'The road forks just ahead,' he explained. 'Route Seven goes off to the right and Route Five, which eventually becomes Route Six—just to make things awkward—to the left. They join up again at Lyons over two hundred and fifty miles away.'

'So it doesn't much matter which one we take,' Jane said as she leaned over his shoulder and gazed at the map with the strange names on it, like Montargis, Montereau, Cosne and Avallon.

'I wouldn't say that,' he replied, 'I've been on Route Seven before and it gets terribly twisty just before you reach Lyons. Hairpin bends for mile after mile.

Route Six looks a bit longer but I bet it's the quicker way.'

The 'back-seat drivers' had been listening attentively. 'I vote for Route Six,' Jacky said.

'Me too,' Jimmy added.

'Okay, Route Six it is,' concluded Darcy and off they went.

An hour later Bertha rumbled through the narrow streets of Sens, past the ancient cathedral with intricate carvings on its west front. She was rolling merrily southwards through the Yonne valley where cattle grazed in the lush green fields when Jimmy and Jacky suddenly felt a bumping sensation underneath them that occurred at regular intervals and appeared to be getting worse each time. Darcy pulled in to the side of the road and sat still for a moment, his head cocked on one side as though he were straining to hear some faraway music.

'What is it?' Jane asked, glimpsing the look of concern lurking behind his bushy moustache.

'A puncture, I'm afraid,' he replied shortly. He jumped out and inspected the back wheels. 'Yep, I thought as much. It's as flat as a pancake this side. We must have picked up a nail or something. It would happen just here, miles from the nearest town.'

The Three Jays clambered out and inspected the forlorn-looking flat tyre. 'Dashitall, what are we going to do?' Jacky asked.

'Change it, of course,' Darcy said absent-mindedly.

'We can't go another yard with it like that. With these wire wheels, the spokes would push right through and ruin the wheel as well as the tyre if we tried to run on it any distance.'

'Can we help?' came from Jane.

'No, thanks all the same. Jimmy here might lend me a hand but there's not room for more than two on the job. Hell, I've just remembered—I didn't check the spare tyre before we left. I only hope that's not gone flat as well!'

The two girls did help to get the luggage out of the back where of course it was resting on top of the jack and the other tools. Darcy picked up a wrench and began to remove the spare wheel which was fixed to the very back of the car, exposed to the weather. In spite of the grease that was liberally smeared around it and which smartly transferred itself to Darcy's and Jimmy's hands, arms and faces when they paused to rub the sweat off their brows, the wheel nuts had rusted in slightly and it took several minutes of tugging, banging and—on Darcy's part—muttered cursing to pull it free. Darcy prodded the spare tyre with a practised thumb and looked gloomy. 'As I suspected,' he said, 'it's not actually flat but it's jolly soft.'

'Well, why don't we pump some air into it?' Jacky suggested.

'Because we just haven't got a pump,' Darcy mimicked her tone.

The Three Jays looked solemn. This was no joke to be stranded miles from anywhere with one punctured tyre and only a soft one to replace it with. As if to match their sinking spirits, the sky began to cloud over and soon a sharp rain-shower came scudding down on them. Pandemonium set in. Darcy had the jack set under the back axle and didn't dare move in case it slipped. He shouted instructions to the Jays to raise the folded hood and screw it on to the supports on either side of the windscreen. They wrestled and tugged at the stiff joints of the hood which began to billow under the pressure of the wind when at last they had raised it from its bed. The rain was sweeping down the road and drenching them. Jimmy, scuttling round the back to lend a hand to Jacky who looked as though the hood might lift her any minute instead of vice-versa, accidentally trod on Darcy's hand. Darcy nearly burst a blood vessel in his efforts to restrain himself. At last the hood was in position and the two bedraggled girls crept in under its shelter while Jimmy went back to help Darcy.

Finally, they managed to change over the wheels, gingerly lowered the jack and straightened their aching backs. The rain had stopped as suddenly as it started but Darcy and Jimmy were already soaked through, their shirts clinging damply to their bodies. (They had taken off their jackets when they set to work.) Their hands and wrists were black with oil and dirt and there were smears on their faces. Jimmy's shirt front, which had been snowy white and a credit to any detergent when he had left Miserden that morning—or was it an age ago?—now had a grimy handprint across it.

Jacky and Jane gazed at the other two standing limply outside the car. Their mouths twitched, their shoulders began to shake and then they burst out with peals of laughter. Darcy scowled for a moment and then he too, glancing at Jimmy's and his own appearance, weakened and joined in. In a moment all four were consumed with helpless laughter.

Jacky pointed at Jimmy's shirt and managed to stammer, 'If you—only knew—how funny you look. The sign of the black hand!'

'You can't talk,' Jimmy retorted. 'You look as though you'd been left out in the rain!'

'Well, weren't we?' At this sally they all roared again. It took several minutes before they sobered down.

'We'll have to smarten up somehow,' Darcy said at last, 'before we find a hotel for the night. No one would take us in looking like this. Here, Jimmy, better get your coat on quickly. It'll hide the stain and stop you catching a chill with that wet shirt. And let's wipe our hands on the grass, to get the worst of the muck off. I've got a spare pair of driving gloves somewhere. You'll have to wear them when we go into a hotel so that nobody can see the state of your hands!'

'Are we going to stop for the night soon?' Jane asked.

Darcy nodded. 'I reckon we're about twenty-five miles from Auxerre and we'll have to take it very gently with this soft tyre. I daren't risk going too far and we'll have to get both tyres fixed before we push on tomorrow. Besides, we've been on the road nearly twelve hours and done well over three hundred miles. If we cruise on to Auxerre and stop the night there, we'll have broken the back of the journey.'

'How far will we still have to go after that?' Jacky asked.

Darcy studied the map and struggled with some mental calculations. 'It's just on five hundred miles from Paris to Marseilles and Auxerre's about a hundred miles south-east of Paris—say we've got four hundred miles to go and you won't be far out. That means, barring accidents, we can stop tomorrow night somewhere in Aix en Provence, pick up Pat from Marseilles Airport at crack o' dawn and drive together to the Camargue. Okay, let's see whether Bertha can limp another few miles. If you could shift the luggage to the other side of the car and you, Jacky, come and sit in the front with Jane, it'll take some of the weight off the bad tyre.'

The passengers rearranged themselves, Darcy started the engine and drove gingerly down the road.

Without further incident they passed through the long tunnel where the road had been drilled through the side of a steep hill near Joigny and, half an hour later, crossed the bridge at Auxerre. Darcy pulled up in a side street just off the main square.

'What's the matter now?' Jacky queried.

He smiled a little sheepishly and said, 'Nothing—really. The thing is I'm going to look a bit stupid when we call at a hotel here and ask if they've got rooms—specially if Jane has to do all the talking and I just have to stand there like a clot. Come on, Jane, you tell me what to say now and I'll learn it off by heart.'

'But I thought you were hot stuff at the lingo,' Jane said innocently. 'Remember how you blinded that gendarme with science just after we left Le Touquet this morning?'

'Come off it,' he replied. 'Dash it all, a fellow can have a little joke, can't he?'

Jane relented after some more teasing and taught him two or three simple French sentences. Guessing that the receptionist might be a woman, she told him to end up with, '*Je crois que tu es belle.*'

'What does that last bit mean,' Darcy asked suspiciously. *Belle* means "beautiful", doesn't it? Hey, you're not pulling my leg, are you?'

Jane and the others managed to keep straight faces, as she replied airily. 'Of course, it does. That last bit only means, "Hasn't it been a lovely day?" Our

French mistress at school always says that the French are a very polite race and they like to talk about the weather—the way we do.'

'Fair enough', said Darcy as he drove on towards the nearest hotel. They all got out and, with Jimmy in the background keeping his dirty hands out of sight, they trooped up to the reception desk. Darcy drew a deep breath and, in an accent which Jacky later described as that of an Eskimo with a cleft palate, blurted out to the middle-aged, severe-looking woman at the desk, '*Bon soir, mademoiselle. Avez-vous deux chambres, une pour le garçon et moi et l'autre pour les deux jeune filles ici? Je crois que tu es belle.*' He smiled at the woman, as much as to say, 'There, you never thought I'd do it, did you?'

The receptionist drew herself up straight, gave Darcy an icy glare and replied in faultless English, 'I do not wish to hear personal remarks about myself. Yes, we have two rooms vacant—kindly fill in these cards and the porter will show you up.' She banged the bell on her desk imperiously and a man in uniform came forward to take their bags.

'Bit of a tartar, isn't she?' Darcy murmured when they were safely out of earshot. 'What did I say wrong? I said exactly what you told me to, didn't I, Jane?'

'Oh yes,' she replied. 'You did it very well!'

'Perhaps she isn't interested in—in the weather,' Jacky said softly.

[65]

After a thorough wash and a tidy up, they decided to have an early supper when Darcy had arranged—by sign language, mainly—for the garage next door to the hotel to mend the punctured tyre and pump up the other. It had been a long day and by nine o'clock the Three Jays were fast asleep in bed while Darcy sipped a brandy in the lounge, cowering behind a French newspaper which he didn't understand in order to avoid the cold stare of the receptionist who looked right through him whenever their glances met. The Jays had somehow failed to enlighten him on his innocent *faux pas*—which was just as well for their state of health!

Next morning, after a breakfast of hot croissants and coffee in their bedrooms, the four were away early while the dew was still fresh. Bertha, now sound on all four legs, as the horsey-minded Jacky put it, bounded along merrily, rolling up the long carpet of miles beneath her proud radiator. They had a picnic lunch just outside Mâcon, and in the early afternoon, drove through that great engineering feat, the gleaming road tunnel which seemed to run for miles under the heart of the big city of Lyons.

South of the city the weather seemed to change mysteriously. The skies were a lighter blue, drained of colour by the blazing sun. The landscape was brown and parched-looking and only the dusty green of the vineyards alongside the road gave relief to their eyes, screwed up against the glare of the sun.

The Jays were grateful now for the fact that Bertha was not a saloon car, as the breeze from her speed caressed their bare arms and necks.

Further south they went, through Valence and Montelimar—where almost every shop, including filling stations, seemed to sell the famous local product, nougat. Inevitably they stopped, unable to decide to just which of the neatly decorated shops they should give their custom. For the next forty miles while Bertha raced alongside the muddy-brown Rhône, as far as Orange with its Roman arch bisecting the road, the Jays were unusually silent, their mouths jammed with hard nougat, soft nougat, nougat with almonds in it, fruit nougat—in fact, every kind of nougat which the native wit of the French could devise. They stopped for a few minutes at Orange to have a look at the immense Roman theatre there.

'You wait,' said Darcy. 'This part of the country is full of the terrific feats of Roman architects. I can't imagine how they found enough people to fill all their theatres and arenas with seating capacity for thousands. Dash it all, we've only seen vineyards and olives for miles and that wouldn't keep many people alive for long.'

'I know,' said Jacky, 'beer's more your line, isn't it?'

'Whack-oh,' laughed Darcy.

He drove on until in the late afternoon they came to the ancient walled city of Avignon.

'Can we drive over the bridge where the folks dance in the song "Sur le pont d'Avignon"?' asked Jane.

'Stupid,' Jimmy said smugly, because he had been doing Southern France in geography at school. 'We haven't got our bathing costumes on and besides Bertha isn't amphibious—she even splutters after being in a thunderstorm, let alone after a swim in the Rhône.'

Jacky looked puzzled. 'What in the world are you gabbling about?'

'Wait and see,' Darcy replied as he carefully threaded his way through the narrow streets, Bertha taking up far more room than was comfortable for any pedestrians sauntering along.

'Goodness, is that the Pont d'Avignon?' gasped Jane as they came round a corner and looked down on to the Rhône. 'It's only half a bridge. Gosh, we'd look funny driving off the end of that on a dark night!'

They made a little tour through the city and saw the Palace of the Popes where they had to make their home during the fourteenth century in the 'Babylonish Captivity'.

Jacky, well educated in the vintage and names of wines, remarked, 'Now I know why that good red wine is called "Châteauneuf du Pape", it must have got its name when the Popes were in residence here.'

Darcy decided that they ought to be getting on

their way and he tore them away from the fascinating and historical city. They hung over the back of the car watching the great walls disappear as Bertha put the distance between them.

From Avignon to the University town of Aix en Provence, the children gamely fought a losing battle against going to sleep. Darcy covered the last lap of the journey in record time, as he wanted to see a flying friend of his who lived in Aix and perhaps get him to have dinner with them. Jane was encouraging his use of a few French words, in fact the four of them had a competition as to who could make the most French sounding sentence. Jacky got the booby prize with '*J'éspère qu'on arrivera bientôt parce que* I'm full of Aix and pains after this long drive.'

'Courage, *mon choux*, we'll be Arles right tomorrow morning,' drawled Jimmy in his would-be American accent as a reply.

'*Tiens, tiens*,' said Jane, screwing up her face in an agonized expression. '*Je crois* that your puns are terrible.'

Luckily at that moment they drove over a brow of the hills and saw Aix en Provence ahead. The sun was already dipping westwards as the dust-stained Bertha came slowly into the main tree-lined avenue. Banners across the street announced that an exhibition of Picasso's paintings was in progress.

'Remember the first time you ever came to

Miserden?' Jimmy reminded Jacky. 'And what you said about Pat's etching by Picasso?'

'I remember you thought Picasso was a floor-polish,' Jacky retorted, blushing a deeper red underneath her new sunburn. She had been a thoroughly spoiled child in those days but it had not taken her long to respond the right way to her new friends' leg-pulling.

Many visitors had been attracted to Aix by the exhibition and Bertha had to twist in and out through several of the narrow streets, where medieval houses leaned against each other, before they finally found a hotel with vacant rooms. By now Darcy had got over his wish to shine as a French scholar and he firmly deputed Jane to do all the talking. He still could not quite understand his frosty reception at the hotel in Auxerre the night before. Nor were the Jays prepared to enlighten him!

At dinner that night with Darcy's friend proving himself even quicker off the mark for leg-pulling than the three Jays themselves, the spirits of the whole party were bubbling over. They had successfully travelled over seven hundred miles from Miserden to Aix in two days and already the events *en route* were becoming something to laugh about.

CHAPTER 4

White Horses, Black Bulls

I LEFT Miserden about the time that Darcy, his
friend and the Jays were having their gay dinner
in Aix en Provence. While they were watching
the University students wandering through the
pretty little squares each with its fountain in the heart
of the old French town, I was watching the lights of
London disappear as my plane took me to Paris.
The next morning after changing planes, I arrived at
Marseilles dead on time and there were the Jays and
Darcy waiting for me at the airport. It was almost
too good to be true that we had all met up as arranged
so far away from home.

I was suitably greeted as the long lost cousin, after
our separation of three days. I noticed that they all
had quite a tan on their faces from the drive in an
open car. We wasted no time in getting on our
way for the Camargue, and decided to take the
coast road to Arles, to keep away from the main
traffic.

The first excitement was a view of the blue Mediterranean as we drove west from Marseilles across
the flat sandy land to Martigues. Here we had some
coffee sitting outside a little restaurant on the central

island, where we could watch all that was going on.
The Jays were fascinated with the fishermen and the
boats on each side of the bridge.   On one side the
boats went out to the Mediterranean for sea fishing
and the other side led to the inland lake of the Etang
de Berre with its freshwater fish.   Festoons of nets
hung on the walls of the houses, topped by washing
strung across the narrow streets.   Some of the men
working on the boats and mending the nets looked
as swarthy as Arabs.

After this break we sped on to Arles across La
Crau, the flat stony plain grazed by scruffy looking
sheep and goats.   Turning on to the main Salon-
Arles road, we drove slowly past the Roman wall
which still circles part of the town and into the centre
of Arles.   Darcy took Bertha into the central *Place*
so that we could have a look at the lovely old stone
doorway of the Portail de St. Trophime.   Jacky
wanted to get a film for her camera and put on her
most charming smile as she asked me, '*S'il vous plait*,
could you possibly lend me just a few francs.'

'A few wouldn't go very far, madame,' I laughed
and within five minutes my store of francs was sadly
depleted because while Jacky got her film, Jimmy
had spotted a little model of a fighting bull and Jane
had picked out another plastic ornament of a Gardian
mounted on his grey horse holding a trident in one
hand, while his girl sat behind him on the horse's
croup.   The shopping done, Bertha took us around

the outside of the great Roman arena, which had big notices plastered up advertising the bull fight to be held on the next Saint's Day.

We were expected at the *mas*, as the central farm-house of each estate is called in Provence, at lunch time. It was after mid-day, so we left Arles, crossing the temporary bridge over the Petit Rhône built in place of the old bridge blown up during the war. Winding our way between the high banks of the dykes, we passed rice fields and vineyards. Then, turning down a narrow earth road with deep ditches on either side, Bertha nearly shied off the near side bank as Darcy, at the wheel, spotted some grey ponies in a paddock to the right of us, trotting over to investigate the big green Bentley.

The cries of delight from the three Jays, especially when they saw two cheeky little foals playing together, were no comfort to Darcy, who was certain that the boldest of the ponies would jump the ditch and land in the car!

'If I'd known that I'd be surrounded by horses before I even arrived at the house, I'd have flown you people in and dropped you by parachute,' Darcy snorted. In answer, a lovely grey stallion, watching the car suspiciously, extended his fine nostrils into a trumpet and blew an echoing snort at us across the ditch.

Beyond the field, hidden in a clump of trees, stood the house and farm buildings. We drove between flowering shrubs and up to the steps at the front of the stately *mas*. Bertha never could make a silent arrival, so before we had pulled up, Monsieur and Madame had come down the steps to greet us.

Introductions and hand shaking were scarcely over, when I suddenly bent down and slapped my ankle. 'My friends, the mosquitoes of the Camargue, have wasted no time in having a taste to see if my blood's changed since I last visited you.' It was no joke and Monsieur kindly remarked that they still had the bottle of mosquito repellent that I had left behind last time. Their family seemed immune to the bites, probably because the mosquitoes gorged themselves so much on my rare visits that their appetites were assuaged for life.

'*Voullez-vous voir les chevaux avant le déjeuner?*' Monsieur asked Darcy. Darcy had no idea of the question and seeing Monsieur looking at him, he nodded and smiled. His smile suddenly froze as he realized that *chevaux* were horses!

'I say, I'm terribly sorry but I have to be in Marseilles for lunch. Well, a late lunch,' he added apologetically.

'Only just in time,' I remarked to him quietly. 'Another five minutes and you'd have found yourself on the grey stallion.'

Darcy quickly got into Bertha and waved goodbye. As he started off he shouted back, 'See you Friday, if those wild horses haven't eaten you in the meantime.'

The dust settled on the drive again and peace descended on the countryside as Bertha's vibrating mechanical horses took the tough old car noisily back to Marseilles.

Lunch did not have to be punctual, as time had ceased to rule our lives. We wandered out to see the strong little horses of the Camargue that were being used every day to do the rounds on the estate. Monsieur explained that the horses of the Camargue were always white and the bulls were always black. The cattle bred on these salt marshes were of an old fighting breed, very fierce and wild. They were used for fighting in the *courses de coquarde*, which differed from the Spanish bull-fights in that the men could get killed but never the bull. In fact the fiercer the bull, the more valuable he was to his breeder, who could demand great sums of money when his bull was wanted for *les courses*.

The Jays were listening entranced to this talk of Wild West life and begged to hear more of the work of the Gardians who looked after the land and animals of the Camargue. Monsieur was pleased with their terrific interest and asked me in French if we would like to ride with him to another of his farms after lunch. I could see from Jane's eyes that she had understood the question and I knew there was nothing that the others would like to do better.

We had an excellent lunch, entirely from food grown on the estate, a paella of rice and chicken, fruit and their own *vin ordinaire*, which the Jays drank diluted with water.

By the time we went out to get the ponies quite a wind was blowing and the dust stung our eyes.

'The mistral,' sighed Monsieur, 'an inheritance of the Camargue.' He spoke fondly of the wind, as part of his life and upbringing, which together with the mosquitoes were the two curses of the Camargue. Yet to the local people it was a protection from their precious land becoming overrun and spoilt by tourists. In fact the mistral and mosquitoes safeguarded the privacy of the Gardians. Their land and animals are their absorbing interest and matter far more to them than tourist money. Like most hardworking people brought up in the tough life of the open air, they have fine characters and a great sense of humour.

The horses were driven into a yard, where five of them were selected and caught. They seemed fairly wild and none were shod. Monsieur explained, 'We never need to shoe them because we ride over dirt roads or sand most of the time.'

'Why in the world do we bother to shoe our horses then?' asked Jane. 'I mean the ones that don't have to go on the roads much.'

'Well, there is a difference,' I explained. 'In this dry climate the horses' hooves are always much harder than in England; because at home their hooves absorb moisture from the air and the ground,

which makes the horn softer. We always notice how
the show jumpers' hooves begin to harden after being
in a dry climate for a little time, such as Spain or
parts of America.'

Meantime Jimmy was helping one of the men with
putting on a thick folded blanket on each pony and
a saddle with a high pommel and cantle, like the
Western saddles.

'Once I'm in that one, I'll never fall out,' said
Jacky, looking in astonishment at her saddle.

Jimmy, who had ridden in a Western-type saddle
before, warned her, 'There'll be no riding with your
knees up around your neck in a jockey-cum-show-
jumper monkey-up-the-stick style! You'll have to
be a cowgirl now, Missee Field Ma'm, riding with
practically straight legs and reins in one hand,
neckreining to turn.'

Jacky looked dismayed; she did not want to appear
a fool the first time out in a foreign country but she
had never had the chance to ride polo ponies. The
style she used for her riding, show jumping and
hunting was different from the riding suited for
working cattle.

Instead of the usual bit, the ponies had a hackamore with the pressure low on the nose and nothing
in the mouth. The inside of the noseband was
stiffly lined and the weight of the steel pieces each
side of the caveson, to which the reins were attached,
made the ponies carry their heads well and flex their

necks when they were pulled up. The young pony that I was riding was more or less at the stage of being broken in and I had a hackamore made of plaited horsehair rope and knotted under the chin. This was more gentle and I could correct the pony's mistakes without hurting it. Young horses always need more pulling about to get their balance than a fully trained horse. The more kindly and comfortably that this can be done, the more the young horses will enjoy their lessons.

The Jays swung themselves up on to their greys with ease, because the ponies were not more than fourteen hands high. Monsieur then showed them that they must be ridden on a loose rein and could turn on a sixpence with just a change of weight. Jacky soon got the idea and was practising swinging her right arm as though she was about to lasso a steer!

All the ponies had a rope tied around their neck and looped on to the saddle, in case the rope was needed for tying them up or any other use. We thoroughly enjoyed our ride, especially as everything was new to us. The dust raised by our cantering was quickly blown away by the mistral. After the wind had dispersed the dust trail it whispered to the cypresses for a moment before busily rushing to the reeds growing near the marshy places and leaving them rattling in surprise and trembling with indignation. Then it sung through the tamarisks and on over the dunes, taking a little sand from here and leaving it there, just like an artist who cannot be wholly content to leave his pictures. Suddenly tiring of them, it blew itself in a whirl out to sea, to be tamed and calmed by the warm blue Mediterranean.

With the wind against us we cantered across the flat country, jumping the irrigation ditches. Sometimes we threaded our way along the tops of the dykes between the rice fields or worked around the vineyards, which were ready for harvesting.

The Jays were in their element and Jacky quickly relaxed and started riding in true Gardian style. The first time she jumped a ditch, the horn on the pommel of the saddle caught her in the tummy but after that she took care to sit straighter and not to bend in the middle. Monsieur was obviously delighted at the way they handled their ponies and they really looked at home as they dodged in and out of the olive trees playing the handkerchief game. Jimmy had his handkerchief hanging out of his pocket and the others tried to steal it from him, the successful thief then taking over the handkerchief.

Monsieur turned to me. 'That game is very like one of the Gardian sports, only they hold a bunch of flowers and the person who snatches the flowers from him takes the bouquet and presents it to his girl friend.'

I had watched some of their games a few years

before and one I could remember was like a cross between polo and rugger, with a bunch of flowers as a ball. The art was in the handiness of the horse and in anticipating your opponent's next move.

After Monsieur had seen his foreman on the other farm, we rode back together along a dirt track to let the horses cool off. The young one that I was riding was not so fresh now as he had yet to muscle up and get fit like the other horses which were in regular work. We talked together about the many things we had seen that day and Monsieur told us a little of the everyday doings of his life that to us were completely new.

Suddenly he turned and said, 'I think you three youngsters can join us in the *ferrade* and help drive the bulls to Les Saintes-Maries. We need them there for the *courses de coquarde* next week-end. It means that you'll have to ride across the Camargue to-morrow and spend Wednesday night in my *cabane* on the shore. We bring the bulls in first thing on Thursday morning and they will be sorted out, rested and fed, before *les courses* take place on Saturday and Sunday.'

This was wonderful luck for us and a great honour for the Jays, as it is a very specialized job to bring in the bulls and certainly not one where children are normally allowed or welcome. I had never seen *les courses* in the Camargue, but I explained what I knew to the Jays.

'Of course *les courses* here are not like a Spanish bull-fight where the matador is the star attraction and the bull the victim. Here in France it's the opposite, with the bull as the big star and the men are amateurs and fight for the fun of it. Sometimes they get killed or badly hurt but the bull is never hurt. He has a rosette or *coquarde* tied between his horns and the men must try to snatch it off him. If they get it, there may be a money prize and the more dangerous the bull, the bigger the prize. It's just too bad for the men who don't get the rosette but get tossed instead.'

'Golly, can I try?' said Jacky the brave.

I looked at her fiercely. 'What! and add nursing you to my other commitments? No, thanks. Anyway, you'll be on the yacht by then.'

'Listen to Matadora Jaquita,' teased Jane. 'Stop press headlines. Famous show jumper, Mlle Field, clears the barrier with the help of brave bull.'

Jacky tried to tip Jane off her pony but Jane was an old hand at avoiding that trick.

'Break it up, children,' said Jimmy sternly. 'If we're invited to do a Gardian's job, you'd better not behave like *les petits enfants*.'

We rode back peacefully to the *mas* as sunset changed the clear sky from blue to orangey red. By the time we had put the horses out and gone into supper, night was falling.

Jane asked me why there was so little interlude of

twilight between sunset and night here. Jimmy answered quickly from his store of knowledge, 'The nearer to the equator the less twilight and dawn, that's why the Poles get light all their summer and dark all their winter.'

'I think you're wonderful, Jimmy.' Jacky made sheep's eyes at him and then dodged upstairs to wash and brush up for supper, giggling as Jimmy pretended to chase her.

The next day we set off after lunch on the long trek across the salt marshes to the coast. The ponies picked their way easily over the clumps of spikey grass and they seemed to know exactly which stretches of shallow water could be splashed through with firm footing underneath and the places to be avoided where the water hid treacherous bogs or quicksands.

'What are all those white birds?' Jane pointed to a sandy hummock surrounded by water with a flock of birds settled on it as peacefully as snow.

'Flamingoes,' shrieked Jacky. 'Remember the Duchess who played croquet with them in *Alice in Wonderland*?'

Her shout frightened the flamingoes and they rose in a great pink cloud as they spread their wings.

'Gosh, how lovely, it's like the aurora borealis,' whispered Jane in awe. The flamingoes settled back like snow on their island and we rode on towards the sea.

Ahead of us we could see the dunes that marked the coast, with the dark *cabanes* crouched against the sandy background. They never seemed to get any nearer, because distance is deceptive on the flat marshes. The outline of Les Saintes-Maries with the church and the bull-ring standing out on the horizon, appeared to move gradually from ahead of us around to our left. Then we could hear the sound of the surf on the far side of the sand dunes and after splashing across one more stretch of water, we arrived at Monsieur's *cabane*. The roof nearly touched the ground on either side but the outside walls were whitewashed like the crofts of Ireland and Scotland. Madame had already arrived by car and through the top half of the door, that opened like a stable, wafted a wonderful aroma of cooking. The Jays turned up their noses like the Bisto kids.

'Fee-fie-fo-fum, I smell something that's good for my tum,' chanted Jacky.

'Hey, you look after your horse's tum before you interest yourself in your nosebag.' Jacky looked at me, licked her lips and then swallowed in a resigned way and turned back to see to her pony.

After turning the ponies into a corral nearby, we walked back along the top of the sand dunes, with the wirey grass stinging our legs. On one side the sea stretched away over the horizon and on the other the flat marshes of the Camargue melted into the skyline. Other than a line of telephone wires

leading to Les Saintes-Maries on the coast to the
north of us, there was nothing to relieve the flatness
and yet the scene was beautiful in its own way.

'Come on', Jane called to me, 'I'm absolutely
famished.' We ran down the dunes to the *cabane*,
Jane arriving last after losing a shoe in a boggy
puddle. We entered the cool and dark interior of
the *cabane*. As our eyes got used to the dim light
after the brightness of the sun, we saw that the almost
circular inside had a dividing wall, which supported
the central chimney and fireplace. The smell of
roasting meat wafted over from the fire where
Madame was turning a spit upon which was impaled
a sizzling bird.

Madame straightened up and smiled, '*Bienvenue*
to our *petite cabane*, though we ladies are honoured
to be allowed to camp here as this is usually my
husband's private hide-out, where he escapes when
he's tired of feminine company and the family
responsibilities!'

'How super this is,' Jimmy said as he took in the
surroundings with old firearms hanging on the bare
walls and the stuffed head of an enormous bull
mounted above the fireplace. Hanging on the
sweeping horns 'as big as cathedrals' were various
ropes and leather thongs.

'Those ropes wouldn't have stayed there long in
that chap's heyday,' said Monsieur who had just come
in and noticed Jimmy admiring the head. 'He was

the fiercest bull the Camargue has had for many years. During his career he killed eight men and he commanded the highest price for *les courses* ever recorded.'

'Eight men,' cried Jacky. 'That's put me off my dinner!'

'All the more for us,' replied Jimmy heartlessly but he too was most impressed by what he had been told and wondered how they were going to fare the next day with the bulls.

I went over to the fire to see if I could help Madame with the dinner. She had everything well in hand. There was a big pan stewing on one side of the fire full of bouillabaisse, a soup of both freshwater and sea fishes, all caught near by. I inhaled a substantial whiff of garlic as I bent down to see how it was cooking. I remembered that chillies and garlic were always a good part of Provençal cooking. At least we were all eating the same thing, which cancelled out the worst aspect of the anti-social garlic eating habit. Garlic is also supposed to stave off colds and flu and I thought that we would be immune for years, as I caught another overwhelming blast from the bouillabaisse.

We settled down crosslegged around the fire, while the soup was ladled out with the tender pieces of fish. We were given hunks of home-made bread for sopping up the soup and we all set to with the appetite given by a day's riding. I noticed that the

Jays became terribly thirsty from the piquant flavour of the soup.

'Wonderful,' said Jimmy as he put his plate down with a contented sigh.

'*Eh bien, encore un peu?*' asked Madame.

None of the Jays could manage any more, especially as they were unaccustomed to garlic. Also, they had their eye on the roasting flamingo on the spit. It had been a victim of the telephone wires but its misfortune was our luck, because one could not wish for more delicious eating. In fact the two proverbial treats of the South African hunters are 'the hump of an eland and the breast of a flamingo.' By the end of dinner we all could vouch for the second.

Jimmy by then had decided that he would like to become a Gardian and Monsieur started telling the three of them many exciting stories of true happenings in the lives of the Gardians. Gradually the effects of the big meal and the dancing shadows of the flickering fire began to tell. The eyelids of the children kept dropping in spite of the efforts to keep them from closing. Mine were doing the same, I must admit.

It was time to get the pile of rugs out and find a corner in which to bed down. The Three Jays and I slept in the second room, with the one little window wide open but shielded by a mosquito net. There was a good through current of air to the top of the front door, which was left open with another net across it to stop the mosquitoes from keeping us awake. It would have taken an earthquake to disturb any of us that night. I woke at the first light of dawn and heard Monsieur and Madame moving around on the other side of the partition. Jane saw me sit up and she woke the others.

The morning was clear and fine with no mistral and after a cup of coffee we went out to get the horses.

'*Un beau jour pour la ferrade,*' Monsieur said with satisfaction. Five minutes later we were riding over the marshes, south of the way we had come the day before. The bulls had already been rounded up by the head Gardian and we were going to help with taking them across the marshes to Les Saintes-Maries.

'Why is the little town called the Saint-Maries of the Sea?' Jacky asked Monsieur.

'Because there is a legend that the Blessed Virgin Mary, Mary Magdalene, Mary and Martha, the sisters of Lazarus, and their servant the black Saint Sarah, together with other friends of Christ, landed there shortly after the Crucifixion.'

'The gypsies come here to pay their devotion to their patron Saint Sarah, don't they?' I asked.

'Yes, they make the pilgrimages in September and May but you'll see plenty of gypsies today and hear the guitar.'

Jane winked at Jimmy, 'We'll never get Pat away from there if people start playing the guitar.'

'*Tienes razón,* dead right,' I said, the Spanish coming naturally with the thought of guitars.

We were approaching a cluster of buildings with a corral nearby and a dust cloud hanging over it, as the restless bulls trampled around in its confining stockade. From the other side two other Gardians were converging on the farm and we all arrived there at about the same time. The head Gardian came over and greeted us on his prancing grey horse, famous for carrying his master through all his greatest triumphs with the bulls.

Monsieur had already explained to us that we had to ride behind and slightly to each side of the bulls to keep them moving in the direction of Les Saintes-Maries.

Steers, trained by the Gardians, had been put in with the bulls to quieten them and to act as nannies and guides on the trek across the Camargue.

We were lined up beside the corral while a man climbed on to the fence and pulled the rope to open the gate. He stayed safely on the fence as the steers cautiously made their way out while the bulls jostled amongst them, fiercely snorting as they left the confining fence.

'*Aha! Ho! Taureau!*' shouted the Gardians, to get them going in the right direction. The men all carried tridents, a three pronged lance, with which they could turn or bring the bulls to the ground if they charged. I had once tried to use a Spanish *garrocha*, which is like the trident, but I had nearly broken my wrist when the bull hit it. A matter of timing and knack that I had not yet mastered! So the Jays and I only carried little rawhide quirts, which we could slap on the saddle to make a noise.

The first kilometre or two was a mad rush, with the Gardians keeping the bulls crowded in with the steers, to try and steady them to a more sober pace.

'They'll be tired before they get to *les courses* at Saintes-Maries,' Jacky called to me, as she galloped on my right, her eyes watering from speeding against the salty wind.

As if it had heard her, one bull propped and turned away from the herd with a swirl of dust as it pivoted.

Jacky's pony anticipated the bull's movement and stopped short, turning to head it back into the herd.

'Sit up and sit tight,' I yelled at Jacky, who had been caught napping and very nearly followed the rest of the herd without her pony. Thanks to the high front of the saddle, she got back her balance and turned the bull back to the others.

'Lucky your horse knows its job, or you'd have found yourself chasing that bull to Paris before you could have turned it. As it was, it nearly had five minutes start on you.' I thought I would put her on her mettle. After all, we had the honour of being allowed to help the Gardians and we should prove that we were capable of doing the job properly or at least as well as possible.

From then on Jacky kept her eyes open and was ready for any emergency. The pace had slowed to a steady jog and we were making our way across the marshes in a cloud of fine dust that moved with us until we reached a stretch of water. Then the drum of hooves changed to a splashing noise, as we kept them moving at the same rhythmic pace.

The tranquillity of the scene was not left undisturbed for long, certainly not long enough to think up a little poem, or words for a 'Gardian's Song.'

Jane had got too far out on the coast side of the herd and was looking at the shimmering sea instead of thinking of the job on hand. Suddenly one of the fighting bulls turned to break away but spotted Jane as he wheeled away from the others.

'*Attention!*' shouted the head Gardian, as the bull gave a bellow and charged straight for Jane. Jimmy turned to look and set his pony in a gallop towards Jane as he took in the situation.

Jane swerved her pony just as the bull reached her and it shot past the pony's haunches. Not daunted by missing its target the first time, it pulled up short and turned after her again. The fighting bulls are athletic and fast, also very fit from their life of fending for themselves on the marshes. Jane was galloping away, looking back at the bull gaining on her. Again she swerved at the right moment, keeping her head and her sense of timing.

Again the bull turned to chase her and it was learning rapidly how to anticipate her dodging. Its horn had touched her pony's shoulder in the last turn and a little patch of blood showed up on the white coat. Jane urged her pony again into a gallop with the bull gaining on her at every stride.

Jimmy, cutting straight over a strip of water, made for the galloping group. The bull's horn was within an inch of Jane's pony as Jimmy reached the near side of the bull. He bent down and took the bull's tail with his right hand, then, like lightning, he yanked it to the side.

The next moment, when the dust had cleared, we saw Jane still galloping and the bull lying on the ground looking dazed, while Jimmy was pulling up between the prostrate bull and the flying figure of Jane.

'Bravo!' shouted Monsieur, as he rode over to the bull to force it to its feet and back into the herd at the point of his trident. 'That's the best bit of "tailing" a bull I've ever seen. *Bravissimo*, Jimmy.'

'How did the bull fall down?' queried Jacky.

When my heart had settled back to its normal beat, I told her, 'I think Jimmy must have pulled its tail to the side at exactly the right moment when all four legs were off the ground in a galloping stride. That put it off balance and it fell as it missed its stride.'

'But how did he know just what to do?' Jacky looked over at her friend as he rode back to join us.

Jimmy overheard her and smiled. 'I studied the technique from the President of Mexico trophy you won in New York, Pat. Do you remember—the statue of the cowboy throwing the bull by the tail.'

'Beginner's luck, I bet,' said Jacky. 'Or else you're just wonderful!' she added, but there was genuine admiration in her voice.

We had our work cut out for the next few minutes to get the bulls going quietly again after this disturbance. Jane had joined us and although she was very calm about her frightening experience, her face was nearly as white as the lather on her pony's neck. Near disasters never happen one at a time and the next moment another bull broke away with Monsieur in pursuit. Jimmy, feeling confident of his tactics with recalcitrant cattle, galloped over to help. However, he didn't realize that Monsieur and the bull were skirting a bog. In order to cut off the bull's flight he made straight for the boggy place that looked very little different from the other land he had ridden over. From a flat-out gallop the pony stopped on the edge, as it sensed the danger. Poor Jimmy went flying and landed in the worst place.

Our laughter turned to horror when we saw him begin to sink as he tried to struggle out.

'Quick, a rope,' shouted Monsieur as he headed the bull that had escaped back into the herd. Another of the Gardians galloped over to the edge of the bog and threw the end of his rope to Jimmy. With the rope looped round the saddle horn, the Gardian backed his horse and slowly pulled Jimmy back to solid ground. Meantime Jane had caught his pony and helped her wet and muddy brother into the saddle.

'I do like exciting holidays,' complained Jacky, 'and nothing seems to have happened to me yet.'

'If you'd fallen off, when your pony stopped to turn the bull,' I warned her, 'you'd have found life very exciting sitting on the tip of the bull's horn. Don't you dare take chances. This isn't a game, it's work—and a work that plays with life and death according to luck and the reactions of the workers.'

En route once more, we safely came to the outskirts of Les Saintes-Maries. We hustled through the streets to the bull-ring shouting to the people in the way, '*Attention!*' and to the bulls, '*Aha taureaux! Allez, allez, taureaux!*'

The great wooden door into the yard behind the bull-ring swung shut as the bulls jostled in.

'*Félicitations, mes amis,*' Monsieur beamed at us. 'Very good work.' We patted our horses on their dark necks, caked with sweat and dust. We ourselves did not look much cleaner than Jimmy after his encounter with the bog.

We took our horses to another yard where they were watered and fed and then we were taken to treat ourselves in the same way. I noticed that none of the Jays were walking so freely as they had been two days before.

'Stiff?' I asked Jane.

'No,' she answered promptly. 'Well, a bit!' she added, as she walked up some steps one at a time.

'My sister can only lead with one leg,' mocked Jimmy, noticing how Jane was walking.

'Well, she doesn't want any schooling from you on how to dive into bogs,' said Jacky, standing up for the girls. She too was feeling nearly as stiff as Jane from long hours in a saddle, riding with a different style.

The sight of lunch spread out on tables outside a little restaurant stopped further banter.

I sniffed the air. 'If you three argue after this, your opponent will faint from the perfume of the garlic.'

'A case of first breath strikes opening victory?' queried Jimmy.

'Nonsense,' laughed Jacky. 'First *blow*,' she puffed hard, 'would be absolutely undefeatable.'

By the end of lunch I did not notice many scraps left to show any lack of appreciation of Provençal cooking on the part of the Three Jays.

By four o'clock, the last bit of cheese had disappeared from the plate in front of Jimmy and Madame had arrived with the car to take us back.

The Three Jays had almost forgotten about yachts,

the sea and a week at Cannes and certainly did not
want to leave this friendly atmosphere, with bulls,
horses, gypsies and all the ingredients for so many
adventures. They were woken from their reverie
by Monsieur who lent forward and took Jimmy's
hand, 'Friend, I welcome you to a club, perhaps not
so unique as your Three Jays, but with roots estab-
lished in ancient times. I herewith present you three
people with the badge of the Gardians. May you
be faithful and true members of our honourable
company.'

'*Merci, merci mille fois*, thank you from the bottom
of our hearts,' gasped Jane. Jimmy rose to his feet
and bowed. 'Sir, we will guard this honour with
fidelity and pride.'

Jacky murmured to me ruefully, 'I didn't do much
to earn this.'

'Don't you believe it,' I whispered back. 'We
were the ones who kept the herd together in spite of
all the other distractions!'

The Jays proudly put on their badges and then
Jane suddenly turned to me. 'What about you,
Pat?'

'Ah!' I said turning back the lapel of my coat and
showing the badge with the Gardian's trident up the
centre, securely fastened. 'I am one badge ahead of
you this time and beat you by three years!'

We said a sad goodbye to our friends the Gardians
and a most especial 'thank you' to Monsieur, who

was staying there until after *les courses*. During the drive back to the *mas* the Jays were nearly silent, thinking over their adventurous day.

'I bet Dashitall hasn't had such a whale of a time,' Jacky broke into our thoughts.

But before Darcy arrived the next day, a cable came from Mr. Field. Paddy had forwarded it from Miserden together with a warning to me, 'Home Tuesday essential'. The cable was to the effect that some important business matters had cropped up and he could not leave New York for another week.

I was in a quandary because I had to get to Spain to see the horse and I could not leave the Jays with these friends as Monsieur would not be back from Les Saintes-Maries until after the week-end.

When Darcy and Bertha turned up, we debated together on the problem of how to spend the interim week. None of the Jays or Darcy relished the idea of staying on board the palatial yacht without Mr. Field being there.

It was Darcy who had the brainwave. 'Dash it all, I've got the solution.'

I thought I heard a murmur of 'Rubber solution?' and Jimmy's reply of:

> 'Darcy was a scientist
> Alas he is no more
> For what he took for H_2O
> Was H_2SO_4.'

CHAPTER 5

'Alassio, Here We Come!'

D ARCY was grinning like a Cheshire cat as he repeated slowly and emphatically, 'Yes, I've got a real brainwave. A typically bright idea—if I may say so without being boastful!'

The Three Jays, who had been sunk fathoms deep in gloom, brightened up and Jacky even managed to murmur, 'Big head!' just loud enough for Darcy to overhear. He smiled at her benevolently and went on, 'Hear what it is before you make any comments. When I was in Marseilles, I met a character who'd just spent a holiday further along the coast, over the Italian border in fact. He said there was a place called Alassio, wonderful beaches, first-rate swimming and jolly cheap into the bargain. I can't see us mooning round the yacht for a week waiting for Jacky's pa to turn up. Why don't we drive on to Alassio, spend some days there and get back to Cannes in time to meet my favourite uncle, Mr. Field?'

'It is an idea,' Jacky reluctantly conceded.

'A smashing idea!' Jane added. 'You could use some swimming practice, Jacky!' She ducked to avoid the fist that shot in her direction.

'Let's be practical,' I said. 'Point One—what do you use for money?'

'Simple,' Darcy answered. 'Last night at a casino the intrepid aviator had a run of luck on the red. I've got a foolproof system,' he added modestly. 'Look at the results,' and he pulled a thick wad of franc notes out of an inside pocket. 'There's enough there to last us a week. Anyway, we can always call in on the yacht on our way there and get a sub from the skipper.'

'Point Two,' I said. 'I happen to know that the Italian Riviera is always crowded at this time of year, the height of the season. What happens if you get there and can't find anywhere to stay?'

'We're bound to find somewhere along the coast,' he replied. 'Besides, we could always look up the list of hotels and send a wire to a likely one before we leave here. I've got the A.A. Foreign Touring Guide outside in the car.'

'You've got all the answers, Darcy,' I smiled. 'Well, what do you three think of it?'

'Oh, do let's go, Pat!' Jimmy and Jane entreated me. 'It sounds a fizzing place,' Jacky added.

'All right,' I nodded. 'I'll agree. Look after them well, won't you, Darcy? I ought to warn you that sea water has a strange effect on Jacky. Last time I saw her in the sea, she was ploughing along a few inches under the surface—minus any breathing equipment except her own! And I think you'd better call in on the yacht anyway when you're passing through Cannes, to see if there are any new developments. The skipper could cable Mr. Field for you to tell him your change of plan.'

'Right,' said Darcy. 'Will do. I hate to tear myself away from this delightfully horsey atmosphere—ugh!—but I think we ought to be moving fairly smartly. There's quite a drive ahead—and it may take us some while to locate the yacht in Cannes.'

The Three Jays had already packed their cases, so it only remained for them to say goodbye to their hostess and thank her for such an exciting three-days holiday. Then they bundled their things into Bertha and shot off down the road in a cloud of dust, waving cheerfully as they went.

I won't describe in any detail their drive along the coast and over the border into Italy. Many of my readers will know the route and, for the others, I hope it will be a pleasure to come. Hitting the coast at St. Raphael, Darcy took the Corniche, jinking crazily in a series of loops and bends until it straightened out into the plain a few miles west of Cannes. The Jays were quiet for once, drinking in the splendour of the indescribably blue Mediterranean as the car swooped and turned several hundred feet above its very edge. Stopping at the quayside in Cannes, where the old part of the town with its sidewalk cafés, smoke-blackened fishermen's houses and nets spread to dry in the sun gave place to formal gardens, flower beds, avenues of palm trees and the square, shining blocks of famous hotels, they were lucky enough to spot Mr. Field's yacht, riding at anchor in the bay among a forest of gently tossing masts. Darcy managed to attract the attention of one of the officers by waving and yelling—much to the consternation of the local fishermen—and a motor-boat was sent ashore to fetch him. While he was away for about twenty minutes, the Jays feasted their eyes on the riot of colour around them, the gay blue, red and orange beach parasols, the sun-burnt holiday-makers who lolled underneath and always that blue sea lapping softly at the shining sand. It was as though a holiday poster had sprung to vivid life under their noses.

Darcy returned and jumped into the car. 'Well, that's all organized,' he said. 'It's quite a floating palace your father's got there, Jacky. By the way, he'll be here a week today, according to the skipper. We'd better push on.'

Jane was weakening. 'You don't think we might stop here?' she queried. 'It looks terrific.'

Darcy shook his head. 'Bit too crowded and smart for us,' he said. 'Just look at that stretch of beach—not enough space to bounce a ball on. It's a case of "when Father says turn, we all turn." No, Cannes's a fine place for grown-ups but not for youngsters. Let's press on. You ain't seen nuttin' yet.'

Reluctantly they climbed into the car and drove eastwards, past the palm-groves of Juan-les-Pins, through Antibes and along the sandy plain to the precise and elegant Edwardian splendours of Nice. Three parallel roads led out of the town and Darcy chose the High Corniche winding hundreds of feet up between banks of heather and pine trees where his passengers could catch dizzy glimpses of the sun-reflecting sea far, far below. They passed behind Monte Carlo and, as a tribute to Princess Grace, Jimmy began to croon 'True Love' in what he fondly imagined was a close imitation of Bing Crosby's voice. He halted abruptly when Jacky enquired whether a dose of castor oil would help him!

They hit the coast after a series of breath-catching hairpin bends just short of the Italian border at Menton. Here they had to join the queue of cars waiting to cross and spent a sweltering half an hour crawling towards the barrier alongside a cliff which cruelly reflected the heat of the sun. At last their passports had been examined, French francs changed into lire and Bertha's carnet stamped. A swarthy Italian policeman at the frontier waved them on. Bertha ground her way slowly up the hill and gathered speed as she shot into Italy.

Two and a half hours later, as the sun was dropping low into the western sky behind them, they reached Alassio. Darcy stopped in a little square just behind the sea-front and was lucky enough to find a hotel with two vacant rooms at his first shot. The Three Jays could hardly keep their eyes open after such a long day's travelling through the heat and glare of the sun so, soon after a dinner in which *pasta* figured largely on the menu, they went to bed. Even then, sleep was long in arriving. Behind their closed eyelids there rushed a flickering succession of images of all they had seen that day, like the projecting of a colour film that had gone out of control.

In the next two days they quickly fell into a holiday routine. Their hotel was right on the edge of the sea with its own strip of private beach. Breakfast over, they would lie on the beach after smearing themselves liberally with oil and bake in the sun, dashing into the sea for a swim from time to time. Darcy, whose fair skin turned a lobster red almost as soon as the sun's rays touched it and whose nose was already peeling under its top layer of freckles, sat on a deck-chair in the partial shade of a beach umbrella, carefully studying the cricket-scores in a two-day old copy of *The Times*. Jimmy and Jane were good swimmers for their age but Jacky was still a learner. Amid her inexpert splashing she envied the other two as they swam a lazy-looking crawl out to a buoy a hundred yards from the shore and she gritted her teeth, determined to catch up with their standard. Darcy was also a strong swimmer though a rather clumsy one and he spent a long time in the water encouraging Jacky and trying to teach her over-arm, to go with her somewhat jerky breast-stroke.

After a lunch which usually consisted of ravioli or spaghetti, followed by veal in one form or another and topped off with liberal helpings of grapes and/or peaches (in the case of the Three Jays it was always 'and' without the 'or'), the party trooped back on to the beach for a repeat performance of the morning's sunbathing and swimming, not to mention the most energetic games thought up by Jimmy and Darcy. When the sun dropped behind the tall houses and hotels on the front, they would go back to their rooms and change, then wander through the streets of Alassio, stopping at an open-air café for an ice-cream or a cup of *espresso* coffee.

Running parallel to the beach and just behind the promenade was the ancient part of the town, nick-named 'the Drain' by English visitors because it consisted of a narrow cobbled alley kept permanently shady by the tall buildings on either side. From time to time it opened out into a gay square, then closed up again to its previous cramped and tortuous gait. All along the Drain were shops of every kind. In the late afternoons when a cool breeze whispered between the tall houses, the holiday-makers in their hundreds strolled backwards and forwards, halting to look for bargains and chattering to one another in a babel of languages, in which English and German seemed to predominate.

On the second morning after their arrival the Three Jays and Darcy were on the beach as usual. Darcy's moustache seemed to droop slightly as he peered at the cricket scores in the paper from behind his sun-glasses. Middlesex, his favourite county, was having the worst of the argument against its neighbouring rival, Surrey. Out at sea the white sails of several small yachts were glinting in the sun and, closer inshore, a speedboat was zooming around in circles like an angry wasp. The Jays noticed that it was towing a water-skier and they watched with slight envy the curling wave of foam flung back behind the skis.

'Gosh, I'd love to have a go at that,' Jimmy said, shading his eyes as he peered across the sunlit water. 'It must be a wonderful sensation!'

'It looks dead easy,' Jacky said. 'All you have to do is hang on and keep your balance.'

'That's all—nothing to it,' Jane mocked her. 'I don't think! I'd like to see you doing it, Jacqueline, my dear. First thing you'd know, your feet would be in the air and you'd be ploughing a furrow with your nose!'

'Nonsense! I bet if you can ride a horse, you can keep up on water-skis.'

'Whoever said you could ride a horse, Jacky?' enquired Jimmy innocently. 'My goodness, look! The speedboat's coming this way!'

'I wonder if he's looking for more customers,' Jane said wistfully.

Her query was close to the mark. The pilot of the speedboat, a young man with fair hair and brawny limbs burnt almost black with the sun, pulled up about thirty yards offshore. The skier he was towing let go of the rope which forked into two with a circular hand grip at each end, skimmed on for a few yards from his own momentum like a seagull alighting and then finally sank gracefully into the sea. He squatted in the shallow water, tugged off the skis and waded over to the waiting speedboat. A crowd of bathers began to gather round.

The Jays began yelling at Darcy who looked up from behind his newspaper, his mind still miles away on the green turf at Lord's. 'H'm, water-skiing,' he pronounced and, as though he had settled an important argument, he began to let his eyes drop back to the cricket scores. But the Jays were not having that.

'Can we have a turn, Dashitall?' Jimmy asked.

'Yes, I know we'd be all right,' Jacky pleaded.

Darcy smiled at their enthusiasm. 'I just happen to be a bit of an expert at water-skiing,' he announced. 'As indeed I am at most things,' he added airily, amid boos and groans from his young friends. 'It's not as easy as it looks. You need a sense of balance, strong wrists and stomach-muscles— especially stomach-muscles because that's where all the strain comes and—and—oh, lots of things you kids wouldn't know anything about.'

Jimmy nudged Jane. 'Well, if you're such an expert, Dashitall—and we're sure you are, of course, —why don't you show us how it's done?'

'Yes, come on,' Jane urged him. 'You're so wonderful at sports. I'd love to see a real expert doing it.'

Darcy glared at them suspiciously but they kept straight faces. 'Okay, you wise guys,' he said at last in what he fondly imagined was an American accent. 'I *will* show you.'

He stood up, hitched up his swimming shorts, took off his dark glasses and strode the few paces to the water's edge. The Three Jays trooped after him, wading into the sea until they were up to their waists. By the time they were near the speedboat, Darcy had threaded his way through the crowd of bathers and was deep in conversation with the pilot. At least, it was a one-sided conversation because the brawny young man shook his head and gesticulated in reply to Darcy's voluble flow.

Darcy turned to the Jays. 'No spikka da English,' he said with a shrug. 'These characters are too darn lazy to learn other people's languages!'

'Not like you, Dashitall,' Jane said softly. 'You're such a dab hand at French, for instance!'

Darcy grimaced at her, then turned to the young man and began to demonstrate by sign language what he wanted to do. The young man grinned with a flash of white teeth in his sunburnt face and said, '*Si, si*. One t'ousand lire,' holding up all his fingers and thumbs.

'A thousand lire,' repeated Darcy. 'That's over ten bob! I don't want to buy his beastly boat—I only want a short trip behind it. How long for?' he said to the pilot. 'Dash it all, he can't understand. What's the Italian for "how long"? *Quanto* something, isn't it?'

The pilot seemed to understand for he grinned again and imitated someone falling into the sea.

'Until I fall off, eh?' said Darcy. 'Boy, you've got yourself a bad bargain! It's going to take you an hour or two to earn that thousand lire. Jacky, be a sweetheart, would you? Nip back to my deck-chair —you'll find a thousand lire note tucked into my sun-glasses' case.'

'What about fetching some more cash, so we can have a go after you?' Jane asked.

'Yes, bring whatever you can find,' Darcy continued. 'Not that you others will need it. It'll be lunch-time before this fluent non-speaker gets rid of me!'

Jacky sloshed off towards the shore while Darcy squatted in the shallow water and wriggled his feet into the rubber suction grips of what he described as 'these oversize pointed shoes.' The pilot started up the engine and kept it idling. He had coiled up the tow-rope and now he tossed it neatly in Darcy's direction.

'I don't see how you ever get into a vertical position,' Jimmy said.

'Simple,' replied Darcy. 'I just lie back with my toes together and the skis pointed upwards and I grip the rope as hard as I can. When the boat draws away, the rope is pulled taut and then in turn it pulls me upright. Nothing to it.'

'As long as you don't let go,' Jane added.

'That's just the point,' said one of the English visitors who was standing near by in the sea and who had overheard their discussion. 'If you do find yourself losing your balance, let go of the tow-rope at once. Otherwise you'll be dragged along behind the boat with your head down.'

Darcy shrugged, as much as to say, 'You can't teach me anything about this.' Jacky had now returned with the money which she handed over to the pilot. He tucked it in to the top of his swimming trunks, glanced round to make sure Darcy was ready, then revved up the engine. The propeller creamed the water in the speedboat's wake and all the spectators drew back, eyes fixed on Darcy.

He lay back in the approved manner, toes together and the points of the skis projecting perhaps a foot. The speedboat suddenly shot away as the pilot opened the throttle. The tow-rope snaked out straight and Darcy's body began to come clear of the sea, drops glistening off his shoulders. He struggled to lift himself vertical and for a split second he described a perfect letter 'Z', arms stretched out in line with the rope, body from shoulders to ankles leaning back against the pull, striving to heave upright. A moment later he had achieved it and triumphantly skated along behind the boat now surging at speed towards deep water. The Jays gave a brief cheer of congratulations.

'Brief' was the operative word. In the first flush of success Darcy relaxed slightly the strain on the rope. It jerked his arms and upper body forward. For perhaps another second he wrestled to regain his balance but it was too late. The skis slid apart, his arms and head were pulled on by the inexorable drag of the racing boat. Darcy, the self-styled expert, crashed into the sea in a welter of foam. As Jacky remarked long afterwards, 'you couldn't tell whether it was the bow wave made by his nose ploughing along the surface or by his handlebar moustache!'

Then the 'expert' made a second mistake. He forgot to let go of the tow-rope. He was hauled along for several yards in a tangle of thrashing limbs. One ski slipped off and floated away on its own. The other waved forlornly in the spray behind him. The pilot, realizing what had happened, cut the engine and, when Darcy felt the pull lessen, he remembered to let go. He managed to kick off the remaining ski and, scarlet-faced with his efforts and with embarrassment, swam slowly ashore.

There was an ominous silence when he rejoined

the Jays. Then Darcy said, 'The first one who utters a crack about me, I will personally drown right here and now!' This was too much for them. They burst out laughing. He looked so unconsciously funny with his proud moustache drooping and dripping seawater. Jane managed to gasp out, 'No comment,' at which they all began to roar again. Darcy himself began to see the funny side. His lips twitched, then spread in a grin and, a moment later, he too was laughing as heartily as the rest.

'Going to have another try?' Jimmy enquired, when he thought it was safe to venture a remark.

'Not on your Nellie. I must be allergic to water-skiing. Mind you, I'm an expert, of course, on fresh water but the sea must be too buoyant for me. That's what it is. It's difficult to adjust yourself.'

'Of course,' Jacky agreed gravely.

'Well, can I have a go then?' Jimmy asked. 'I've never done it on fresh water so I've got no adjusting to do. Besides, we can't let the speedboat man get away as cheaply as that. It works out at about a hundred lire a yard to date!'

Darcy agreed. A few minutes later Jimmy was ready. The speedboat churned up the water as it shot off and Jimmy's body rose out of the sea. He wavered for a moment but kept his balance and settled into the rhythm, scudding over the crests of the waves set up by the boat's motion. Away out to sea he flew, swerving sideways until he was running parallel to the boat when the pilot described loops and arcs.

It was a marvellous sensation for Jimmy. Like galloping at full speed, he thought, only the movement was smoother. He fell quickly into the knack of keeping his balance and although he always kept the rope taut, he had time to realize the full excitement, feel the breeze tugging at his hair and hear the water smacking at his skis. All too soon the trip was over and, as the speedboat turned for home, he could see the beach racing closer. At last the engine stopped and the boat began to drift. Jimmy remembered what he had seen the first skier do. He let go of the tow-rope, planed along for a few yards, then toppled into the water within a cricket-pitch's length of his friends.

'Super,' he yelled when he got to his feet. 'Absolutely super!'

Jane had to try it after that but she found it was not as easy as it looked. She put her skis on in the shallow water and then sat back, keeping her knees between her elbows as the rope tightened. She was told not to lean forward or try to get up on her skis too quickly. The boat started away and Jane found she was crouching on her skis and being blinded by the spray but every time she started to push herself up by straightening her knees, her skis began to wobble and come apart. So she sat down quickly and again became blinded with the spray.

Her tummy muscles and ankles became terribly tired and she felt that the sea was trying to tear off the seat of her bathing costume after she had been dragged nearly a quarter of a mile still in a sitting position. The sea was more choppy offshore and a cascade of waves drenched her face so that she let go of the rope rather than drown in spray. As the motor-boat roared away, busily churning up its foaming wake, Jane sank gratefully back into the sea and rested her aching muscles, the wooden skis keeping her afloat with the minimum of effort on her part.

No peace for the wicked, thought Jane as the boat turned and came back for her. The pilot threw her the rope and lined up the boat again. She found it much more difficult to start in deep water but was determined to stand up this next time and get clear of the spray. Off went the boat again when Jane had drifted a bit to one side. However, as the rope pulled her, she straightened up and tried to stand. Unfortunately she attempted to jerk herself to her feet and, as she came upright, she bent her elbows, lost her balance and dived forward straight between her skis.

On the third attempt she was more cautious and stayed in the sitting position until she felt ready to stand slowly. Carefully, she kept a steady pull on the rope and tried to relax her knees so that the skis could bounce over the little waves and lines of wake. Successfully the boat towed her back to the shore. She was tiring as they came in and was very ready

[113]

to let go the relentless rope and sink back into the comfort of the sea.

'Not bad for the first time,' said Jimmy kindly. He was also quietly thinking to himself, Thank goodness there are still some sports that boys can do better than girls, even at the first try.

Jacky stood and watched Jane's progress with a twinge of secret envy. She wanted to emulate her friends, though she knew in her heart of hearts that she could not swim well enough to risk falling in when a long way out to sea. She asked Darcy half-heartedly whether she might have a go but, firmly though sympathetically, he shook his head. Jacky clenched her teeth and went off to practise her swimming, doggedly ploughing along with her jerky breast-stroke, determined to catch up with the other two in swimming as she had done in riding.

That afternoon they decided to take a boat trip to the island of Gallinara. About two miles east of Alassio and perhaps a mile offshore, the conical island projected abruptly from the sea. It rose to some four hundred feet or so and dominated the horizon. From the moment they first set foot on the beach, the Three Jays could hardly help noticing it and they were naturally curious to know more. When they learned that motor-boats made regular runs in the mornings and afternoons to take visitors ashore, they persuaded Darcy to leave his days-old cricket scores and accompany them to the island.

Just before three o'clock they paddled through the surf and clambered on to the motor-boat, paying five hundred lire apiece to the swarthy boatman who helped them aboard. Punctually on the hour, the engine clattered into life, the boatman's mate made a wailing noise on the siren and the boat chugged away.

There were a dozen or so passengers aboard, mostly middle-aged Germans whom the Jays studied covertly. The men mainly wore khaki-coloured jockey caps and overlong shorts covering their knees. Each of them carried a camera and they conversed in solemn guttural tones. They seemed to be taking the trip very seriously, more as an earnest duty for the Fatherland than a jolly cruise. After a while the Jays wanted to giggle, so they turned their attention to Darcy.

'I wonder you didn't ski along behind the boat,' Jacky said. 'You're such an expert, after all.'

'Ha-ha,' he answered amiably. 'How about changing the record, Jacky?'

'Talking of records,' Jimmy said. 'I wonder if anyone has ever swum out to the island? It shouldn't be too difficult—if you started from the nearest point on the shore. It doesn't look more than a mile.'

'Hard to say,' Darcy said, shading his eyes from the glare of the sun on the dancing white-flecked waves and gazing at the approaching island. 'See how the waves swirl and seem to change direction just the other side of the island? There must be a tricky cross-current round there. You might have to take it at an angle to allow for the drift and that could almost double the distance. Frankly, I wouldn't like to tackle it for fun.'

Two or three other boats from different parts of the beach were now converging on the island. Their boatmen steered them into a kind of queue and, in line astern, began to aim at a point on the shore side. The grim brown rocks tumbled precipitously towards the sea but the Three Jays could just pick out a man-made wall which formed a small jetty. When the boat was fifty yards away from the jetty they spotted a narrow opening between two huge rocks through which the leading boat steered. When their turn came, the boatman cut the engine and drifted towards the opening. The mate leapt lightly into the water and, hauling on a tow-rope, waded through the dark-shadowed gap, pulling the boat behind him.

Around the corner, the wall and the rocks made a tiny cove, where already the leading boats had tied up and disgorged their chattering loads. The sun beat down fiercely and its rays seemed to bounce off the rocks and the shallow water inside the harbour. The breeze was shut away so that within a few moments the Jays and Darcy felt they were baking in an oven.

'What's the form now?' Darcy queried. 'Dash it all, I'm done on one side already!'

'There's a path leading up to the top of the island over there,' Jimmy announced. 'I vote we climb it. At least, there'll be some shade and some fresh air up there.'

'Yes,' said Jane, 'and there's an old building that looks like a fort at the very top. You could see it on the way out. We might explore it.'

Darcy groaned. 'It looks mighty steep to me from here.'

'Well, it's all downhill on the way back,' Jacky argued.

'Next time I go on a holiday abroad, I'll borrow a bicycle and join in the *Tour de France*,' Darcy said. 'It'll be a jolly sight more restful than tagging along with you kids! Okay, you win—just let me get my alpenstock and I'll clamber up that precipice with you.'

They found out that the boat would leave on the return journey in an hour—at half past four. They set off up the dusty path that wound its way in and out, clinging to the side of the cliff. Soon they outstripped the Germans who were solemnly trudging along, intent on methodically squeezing every ounce out of the holiday experience, no matter at what physical cost.

There were carob trees and gnarled olive trees perching precariously on the cliff on each side of the path. Occasionally a lizard darted across the rocky boulders when it heard them approaching. Close to the summit they found a ruin that looked like a chapel and above it the circular tower of the fort. The four friends walked through a walled enclosure and scrambled up a wooden ladder inside the fort until they emerged at the ramparts.

The view was magnificent. South of where they stood the cliff side fell almost sheer down, down four hundred feet and more to where the aquamarine sea lay in wait. Over their shoulders Alassio was a dark smudge along the coast. The wind swirled around the fort, beckoning them secretly to join it and glide down, like the seagulls that were sailing and swooping round the cliff face beneath. Jacky shivered.

'I wonder why I always get the urge to throw myself over when I'm up on a height,' she said.

'Well, if you're going to,' was Jane's brutal answer, 'bags I your best riding kit when we get back.'

'And can I have Pickles?' her brother chimed in.

'Vultures!' she retorted.

Darcy decided to break up the growing squabble. 'That's odd,' he said, pointing downwards. 'Can you see that enormous shelf of rock jutting out? It makes a kind of right angle with the edge of the island. See it? With that great shadow it throws on the water.'

The Jays peered over the side of the fort. 'Yes, it's plain enough,' Jimmy answered. 'What about it?'

'I only thought it looked as though it was man-made. The rock is so sheer and it must weigh hundreds of tons. It'd make a wonderful natural harbour.'

'The water looks very deep—and almost black from here,' Jane said. 'I'm not sure I'd fancy swimming near that rock. You'd never know what big fishes were hiding in the shadows.'

'Nonsense,' Jimmy scoffed. 'It only looks black because it's in the shade. And don't forget you'd look far bigger to a fish than it would to you.'

'Tell that to the sharks,' said Jacky.

'There are no sharks in the Mediterranean, silly!'

'Maybe,' Jacky cracked back, 'but there are octopuses.'

'Don't you mean "octopi"?' said Jimmy in a lordly way. 'Anyway, they're not fishes.'

'What are they then? Anything that swims in the sea is a fish.' This came from Jane.

'Then you must be a fish—and a pretty poor fish, too!' was Jimmy's swift answer.

Darcy's fears that the Jays might come to blows and knock one another over the narrow ledge slap into the hungry sea so far below were allayed by the arrival of some German tourists who puffed and panted up the vertical ladder on to the ramparts of the fort. There were five of them in all, two men with their wives and a third man who had joined up with the others but who was apparently just a casual acquaintance. While the two couples gravely pointed out the different views to one another and posed in turn to be photographed for the family albums, the third man stood aloof, looking inscrutably at the sea far below through his dark glasses.

There was an air about him that caught Darcy's secret attention. He stood erect and there was a sense of controlled power in his muscular brown arms and legs, like a coiled steel spring. He was bareheaded and his greying hair was cropped close to his skull. Darcy noticed that he wore a black silk glove on his left hand which seemed to be contorted like a claw. He looked like a man who was accustomed to command others and Darcy recalled war-time pictures he had seen of German generals in their peaked caps. There was the same atmosphere about him of ruthless purpose, as though all the softness had been ground away by years of hard will-power.

Darcy gave a mental shrug and inwardly laughed at himself for being fanciful. The man was probably a pork-butcher from Hamburg who had never been in action. Appearances could often be deceptive. He had been reading too many war books lately, he supposed. Glancing at his wrist-watch, he turned to the Jays who had now forgotten their recent argument and were, as usual, discussing the horses of the Camargue quite peacefully.

'Time we were going back,' he said. 'We don't want to miss the boat and have to prove Jimmy's theory that you can swim ashore from the island.'

As Jacky had remarked, it was all downhill on the way back and they reached the tiny harbour within ten minutes. The sun was still beating down and concentrating all its heat in the cove, so that it was a relief when at last the boat was full and the mate repeated his towing act to get them clear of the narrow entrance. During their absence he and the boatman had rigged canvas sheeting along the sides of the boat and the passengers soon realized why. The boatman steered a course straight back towards the shore and, as they cut across the current and the wind, big waves slapped against one side of the boat, flinging up spray that even splashed over the top of the canvas. There was no sign of the solitary German who must have been returning on one of the other motor-boats.

When they met at the breakfast table next morning, Darcy was bubbling with excitement. He could hardly sit still and he kept on drumming his fingers on the white table cloth. 'Hurry up,' he said to the others who had no need of being urged on when there was the prospect of food. 'I've been waiting for you for hours.'

'What's up?' Jacky asked, stifling an early-morning yawn.

'Plenty,' he said. 'After you'd gone to bed last night, I had some coffee with one or two local characters.'

'Only coffee?' Jane enquired innocently.

'Well, a spot of *vino* too, of course.'

'Of course,' they said in chorus.

'Look, do you want me to tell you this or not? It so, button up those flapping mouths, willya?' he went on, copying Jimmy's phoney American accent. Then reverting to his normal speech, he said, 'You remember our trip yesterday? Well, *there's treasure hidden on the island!*'

CHAPTER 6

Treasure-bent

IF Darcy believed you could impress the modern teen-ager with talk of a 'treasure island', he was due for a rude awakening. The Jays looked at his earnest face and then started to laugh.

'Come off it, Dashitall,' Jacky said.

'I've never heard anything so corney,' came from Jane. 'Treasure hidden on Gallinara indeed! You mean to tell us that thousands of people come here on holiday every year—not to mention all the local fishermen who are here all the time—and no one's bothered to find treasure on a small island staring them in the face.'

'I wonder what was in that coffee you drank last night—apart from the coffee!' was Jimmy's contribution.

'Okay—go and laugh your silly heads right off,' Darcy said sharply. 'Don't wait to let me tell you the details.'

'Nine o'clock in the morning's a bit early for a bedtime story,' Jacky answered. 'But I don't suppose we've got anything to lose by listening. What do you think?' she asked the other two.

'All right, we'll buy it,' said Jimmy.

'That's terribly generous of you,' Darcy replied sarcastically. 'Dash it all, I've a good mind not to tell you a thing after that!'

'Oh, come on. We didn't mean to sound rude but really—treasure hidden on Gallinara! You must admit it sounds a bit fanciful.' This was from Jane.

'I should have said "off" and not "on",' Darcy continued. 'Actually, the treasure's not on the island at all.'

'Well, where on earth is it?' Jacky queried.

'It's not on earth either,' he grinned. 'It's in the sea, stupid. Anyway, let me tell you the rumour I heard last night.'

'Now it's a rumour,' Jane observed. 'The way you were talking I thought it was a hard fact.'

'Do you want to hear about it or not?' Darcy demanded.

'Yes,' they said.

'Okay then—just don't interrupt, that's all. You know that open air café just this side of the Drain— the one where they have an orchestra playing and a hunchback who sings? Well, it was pretty crowded last night and I had to share a table with an elderly man and his wife. They were English and they live here all the year round. He must have made a packet and retired young because they had settled here just before the war broke out. They were positive Italy wouldn't come into the war and when they decided to get away, it was too late. They got put in the bag and had a pretty rough time for the next five years, they told me. The Germans pinched their villa and they got herded into a kind of concentration camp with the rest of the English colony who hadn't hopped it in time.'

'I can't see what this has got to do with treasure on Gallinara,' Jacky said. The sea looked so warm and inviting from the dining room window and she was impatient to get on to the beach.

'Hold on, Jacky,' Darcy replied, 'I'm getting to the point. But I've got to put you in the picture first. Anyway, this couple told me that the German commander in charge of the area towards the end of the war was a very tough character. He'd collected a lot of loot from various places, you know, famous paintings, jewellery, gold,—the lot, in fact—and he kept it locked up in a big waterproof box.'

'How did your friends know all this if they were under guard in a camp?' Jimmy asked sceptically.

'Ah, that's just the point. To humiliate the English people, the commander used to make them take turns in waiting at his table, they told me. They used to act dumb and pretend they didn't know any German, although the old boy is a fluent speaker, as he did a lot of business with Germany before the war. They hoped to hear some military secrets which they might pass on in some way or another to the British. And so when the commander used to start bashing the brandy after dinner—which he did most nights—they would stand there looking stupid and keeping their ears pricked. But he never talked about military affairs. He used to send the other officers away and keep only his second-in-command, who was in on the secret. And all the time he used to say how valuable the loot was and they would try to work out private ways for disposing of it.

'Anyway, the war began to take a turn for the worse—for the Germans, that is. The Allies were pushing on beyond Rome and then there was the landing along the coast here near St. Raphael. The Second Front chaps further north were pushing into Germany and this part of the world was pretty well surrounded. The only way out was by sea. One night, just before the war ended, this English couple were waiting on the commander—though by this time he had begun to treat them much better, knowing the game was just about up. He got very drunk that night and nearly had a free fight with his second-in-command. He had whistled up a U-boat from somewhere and it was going to pick him up two nights later off the island—on the far side so that it couldn't be spotted from the shore. He was going to take his precious loot along and leave the second man to stay and fight it out—which didn't go down well with his Number Two. Can't say I blame him either.'

By this point the Jays had shed their boredom and were listening eagerly. Darcy sensed the change in them and went on, 'Now we come to the exciting bit. It seems that the commander got to the rendezvous, which was in the shelter of that enormous rock we looked down at only yesterday afternoon. The U-boat surfaced and came close in as quietly as it could. But it turned out to be one of those midget submarines and the skipper said there was only room for the commander—but not for his heavy box of loot. One or the other could go—but not both! Can't you just imagine his dilemma? If he turned round and went back, the odds were that he and his loot would be captured by the Allies. If he put the loot in the U-boat and took a chance of escaping the British and Americans, he'd never see it again. What a problem! And can't you just imagine them bobbing about off that rock in the dead of night, arguing in whispers so nobody would hear them and the skipper impatient to get away to safety. Anyway, so the story goes, the commander at last made his decision. He decided to save himself.'

'But what about the loot?' Jane demanded.

'Ah, that's the sixty-four thousand dollar question. He dumped it in the sea—just by that big rock!'

'But wouldn't the sea water ruin it?' Jimmy asked.

'No, that's just the point. Didn't I say earlier that he had it in a waterproof chest? He must have thought his only chance was to get himself away and then come back again when things had settled down to dredge up the box.'

'Well, why didn't he?' was Jacky's question.

'Simple. The story goes that the U-boat captain decided to take a chance and travel on the surface to recharge his batteries for the long trip ahead. An R.A.F. plane happened to be doing a dawn patrol along the coast, spotted the U-boat down below and dived on it. Whooomph!' and Darcy flung his hands upwards expressively. 'It was a direct hit—no survivors, although the plane stooged around for a while to make sure.'

'So the loot is still there at the bottom of the sea?' Jane said wonderingly.

'As far as anyone knows,' Darcy answered.

'But I wonder why your old couple have never tried to get it up, seeing they must be the only people to know all about it?'

'That's just what I asked them,' Darcy said. 'They reckon they're too old to be fooling around with boats and diving kit at their time of life. They did give all the facts to the local authorities soon after the war but the Italian boys rather shrugged their shoulders and wouldn't do anything about it. Privately, they probably thought the two old things were a bit screwy after being prisoners for so long.'

'There was somebody else who knew all about it,' Jacky said slowly. 'The German second-in-command—the one who was left behind here to fight it out. What happened to him, I wonder?'

'That's what I asked the people I met last night,'

Darcy answered her. 'They seemed to know all the answers—and they knew this one, too. It appears he was a pretty tough character as well—and brave into the bargain. He could see it was hopeless to try and defend the town itself, so he took to the mountains up there and held out for quite a while with a few picked troops. In the end he was wounded in the hand and captured. My chums of last night said that he was eventually tried as a war criminal for the way he had treated the people here and got sent to gaol for fifteen years. They followed the case very closely, being interested to know what happened to him. Last time they heard, he was in an Allied gaol in Germany.'

'Gosh,' said Jimmy, 'it sounds wonderful. Sunken treasure off Gallinara! You're not pulling our legs, are you, Darcy?' he added wistfully.

'Cross my heart,' said Darcy. 'You couldn't imagine me making up all that detail, now could you?'

'That's a point,' Jane said. 'It sounds too—too right not to be true. It rings true. I can just see that fat old German—I bet he was fat—going out to the U-boat at the dead of night, lugging his precious chest with him. By the way, what do we do with the treasure if we find it?'

' *When* we find it, you mean,' Jacky cut in.

'Hey, not so fast,' Darcy interrupted her. 'No one's said anything about finding the treasure yet.'

'Well, you'd hardly go to the trouble of telling us

all about it if we weren't going to have a good look for it,' was Jane's shrewd comment. 'Oh blow! There's the usual motor-boat going out to the island at eleven o'clock but it doesn't stay long enough for us to do any real searching.'

'Not to mention the fact that the trippers and the boatmen would be more than curious if they saw us poking about by the rocks,' Jimmy added.

There was a smug look on Darcy's face. 'Don't fudge your tiny brains, my children,' he said. 'The expert has got all the answers. Do you remember on our way back yesterday from the island we passed near a kind of yacht basin half a mile or more up the coast? The penny dropped with a clang, I can tell you, when I thought of it this morning—while you were bashing the blankets in your well-known style. I made a few enquiries from the hotel here and nipped along to the place before breakfast. I am now a proud member of the Alassio Yacht Squadron— here's my ticket,' and he flourished a green card which he dug out of a pocket. 'This means I can hire a sailing boat whenever I want one.'

'Do you know how to sail a boat, Darcy?' Jane asked him.

'Do I know how to sail a boat? Why, I've for- gotten more about . . .'

'Please don't say it,' Jacky begged. 'If you're as expert with a boat as you are at French and water- skiing, we'll all get drowned!'

'Anyway, Jim and I have been out with Pat several times, so we'll be able to help,' Jane said. 'Let's start now!'

'No,' replied Darcy. 'This is something we can't rush. We've got to work out a plan of operations first. Let me see now—the morning boat trips to the island leave here at eleven and get there about half an hour later. The tourists spend an hour on the island and leave about twelve-thirty. The afternoon tours leave here at three o'clock and arrive at half past. That means the island is clear for three hours each day. By the way, did anyone notice if there are people living on the island?'

'I'm pretty sure there aren't,' Jimmy answered. 'There was that tumbledown building just below the fort that looked like a ruined church or something but no sign of life round it.'

'All to the good,' Darcy went on. 'Here's my plan. We tell the hotel we're going for a sail and get them to make up a picnic lunch for us. We'll hire a boat and sail off in the direction of the island. That won't look suspicious because I saw a lot of boats sailing round the area yesterday. When we see the last of the motor-boats pulling out around twelve-thirty, we'll nip in and do a recce.'

'The water's jolly deep round that rock, I should think,' Jimmy said. 'Oughtn't we to get some diving gear?'

'Not this first time,' Darcy replied. 'If it looks at

all promising, we can buy some flippers and masks when we get back this afternoon and try again tomorrow. There's a shop along in the Drain that sells all that sort of thing.'

By this time breakfast was over and the Jays were eager to get going on their treasure quest. 'One last thought,' Darcy said, as they were about to spring up from the table. 'Not a word to anyone about the idea, remember. As far as the hotel's concerned, we're just going off for a jolly day on the ocean waves!'

The Jays already had their swimming costumes on under their shorts and shirts and Darcy rushed off to do the same. Jane had a minor brainwave and managed to borrow an inflatable rubber dinghy from the hotel-owner. Collapsed, it would take up next to no room in the boat and, when blown up, would take Darcy alone or two of the Jays at a pinch. It would come in handy if the wind or the rocks prevented the boat from sailing close inshore.

They bundled into Bertha and drove along to the yacht basin where they hired a sixteen-footer, paying a hefty deposit for the privilege. A pair of oars was thoughtfully provided and, as there was almost no breeze in the shelter of the cliffs, Darcy heaved away until they were in open water, grunting that he never thought he'd end up as a galley slave!

Luckily, the boat was simple to operate. There was only a mainsail with a jib and after several false

starts, when the boat yawed dangerously and zig-
zagged like a drunken water-beetle, Darcy got the
hang of the sails. Jacky sat well for'ard and Jimmy
and Jane crouched in the well of the boat, keeping an
apprehensive eye on the boom and ducking smartly
whenever it swung on to the opposite tack. Darcy
handled the tiller and set a course to the west of
Gallinara—at least that was his intention but the boat
seemed to have ideas of its own. It spanked along,
pushing a curling bow wave ahead. The sea slapped
rhythmically against its hull and the waves glinted a
royal blue in the sunshine. Jacky began singing
'What Shall We do with the Drunken Sailor?' and
the others felt like regular sea-dogs as they roared out
the chorus of the chanty.

It was close on eleven o'clock as they drew level
with Gallinara, its grim rocks etched sharply by the
sun. Far off along the coast the motor-boats began
to put out to sea, so Darcy decided to make a wide
circuit round the island in order not to arouse any
suspicions. When the boat was over half a mile
out beyond it, he hauled down the mainsail and
allowed the boat to drift while they ate their picnic
lunch.

Jane trailed her hand in the water and watched a
shoal of minnows nosing after it and trying to nibble
her fingers. Their bodies gleamed golden in the
sunlit water and down through the translucent sea
there were vague, shadowy depths which seemed to

invite her to plunge down and wrest their secrets away. 'How about a swim?' she suggested.

Darcy had just taken an enormous bite out of a sandwich and so, his mouth being too full for words, he shook his head vigorously. When he had swallowed the mouthful, he said, 'Not just now. It's not a good thing to swim right on top of a meal and besides, you'll have plenty of swimming later.'

'Call this a meal?' asked Jacky plaintively. She had only eaten four sandwiches, two peaches and a large bunch of grapes.

'Well, it's all you'll get this side of dinner, so make the most of it,' was Darcy's retort. 'Anyway, while we've got the chance, we'd better do a spot of planning. As soon as the motor-boats leave, I'll bring this craft in as close as I can. We may have to row the last part because the wind could be tricky close to the island and we don't want to pile up on the rocks. Now let me see—who's an expert at under-water-swimming?'

'Jimmy's pretty good,' replied Jane. 'He's done the length of his school baths and that's thirty yards, isn't it, Jim?'

Jimmy nodded and said, 'Jane's not too bad. I reckon she can stay under as long as I can.'

'Now that the mutual admiration society has had its say, it's my turn,' came from Jacky who was looking slightly sour. 'I don't even have to try to swim underwater. I can do it naturally!'

'Yes, but how about coming up to the surface again, old girl?' Darcy asked. 'That's always a good thing, you know. This is the form. I'll go down first and see what I can spot. Then Jimmy and lastly Jane. If we keep to that strict order, everyone will have a chance to get their breath back between dives. But remember, I don't want you to be too ambitious. We're not seeing who can stay down longest.'

The others nodded. Jane, the ever-practical, said, 'There's a spare coil of rope in the boat. Wouldn't it be an idea if we tied it round our waists each time we go down? Then, if anybody got into difficulties, the others could haul him out.'

Darcy smiled his approval. 'That's a bright thought, Janey. We'll do just that.'

Jacky's face had clouded over. 'That's all very well for you three,' she said, 'but what about me? You get all the fun and I just sit here like a stuffed dummy watching you. I wish I could swim well!'

Darcy thought swiftly. 'I've got a very special job for you,' he said. 'We only know vaguely where the chest may be sunk and it could well be close inshore. In any case, it might be easier for us to do our diving from the land side than off the boat. We'll blow up the dinghy and you, Jacky, will have the job of paddling round the little bay, checking on landing places and generally doing a recce. That'll be really useful.'

Jacky beamed with pleasure at being given a responsible task.

The moment the hands of Darcy's watch pointed to half past twelve, he began to erect the mainsail. Far off across the waves, they could hear the faint wailing of the motor-boats' sirens as the little convoy punctually left the island. The sail flapped idly for a while and then the rising breeze nudged it. The boat started to glide through the water and Darcy heaved on the tiller to bring its nose round towards the island. The wind was blowing in gusts straight on shore so that the boat drove a straight furrow in line with its goal.

Within quarter of an hour, they were close under the lee of Gallinara. The steep cliff side loomed menacingly above them and the great rock emerging from the sea, which yesterday they had gazed down on from the fort, now towered above their heads, looking like a gigantic axe blade resting on the floor of the sea, with the sharp edge upwards. As Darcy hauled in the sail, the others peeled off their outer clothes and stripped down to their swimming costumes. The boat edged in towards the angle formed by the cliffs and the rock, which cast a purple shadow across the still water. Time seemed to stand still and there was an infinite, cloistral quiet in the shade of the rock.

Jane shivered. 'It doesn't look quite so inviting from here,' she said in a whisper.

Jacky giggled. 'You don't have to talk softly,' she said. 'There's no one listening—except us.'

'That's the funny thing,' Jane went on. 'I've got the feeling we're being watched from up there.' She pointed almost vertically up the cliff side.

Darcy was pulling off his shirt and he paused with it half over his head to say in muffled tones, 'You're imagining things, Janey. I counted the number of motor-boats going in and coming out—and they were the same each time. And nobody lives on the island when the tourists aren't there.'

'I can't help it,' she said. 'You know what it's like when you're in a room and someone is trying to catch your attention? You can feel their eyes on you and, sooner or later, you look up. Well, that's the feeling I've got now. Look, I saw something flash up near the top!'

Jacky, who had been busy pumping up the rubber dinghy, glanced up, as did Jimmy, who had been tying one end of the rope to the mast. 'I can't see a thing,' he announced. 'Come off it, Jane. We've no time to spare for being dramatic.'

'I'm not being dramatic,' she replied hotly. 'I tell you—I distinctly saw something flash up on the cliff!'

'Probably the sun reflected off a rock,' Darcy said. 'There's a lot of mica in these rocks, I noticed yesterday, and they catch the sun easily. Or it could be an old bottle someone had chucked away up there. There's no sign of life I can see on the cliff. Only a lot of trees and rocks that look as though they're going to fall on our heads any minute!'

He tossed the anchor overboard with a splash that re-echoed off the huge rock. The Jays watched the rope snaking out through the clear water, down, down, down, until at last they could sense the gentle tug when the anchor settled.

'Must be pretty deep just here,' Darcy muttered. 'Okay, let's get started. Jacky, if you've got the dinghy ready, we'll get you away first. Keep us in sight all the time, won't you, and don't take any chances. And if you can land anywhere, do for Heaven's sake pull the dinghy right out of the water. There's no rope to tie it by and we don't want it floating off into the blue!'

She nodded, almost too excited to speak. She wriggled into the dinghy while Jimmy held it steady alongside the boat and then pushed herself clear with the end of the paddle. With short, impatient strokes she made for the rocky water's edge about twenty yards away.

Darcy tied the free end of the rope round his waist. 'Here goes,' he said. 'We'll have to search the bottom methodically, so I'll start with this section. If the rope feels heavy when I come up, you'll know I've found the treasure first time!'

He hit the water with a resounding splash and when the foam had settled, Jimmy and Jane could just see the shadow of his body some fathoms below. The seconds ticked by and they were beginning to feel the cold touch of panic when Darcy burst up into sight, spouting water and sucking in the good air through his open mouth. He swam a few strokes and hauled himself into the boat where he lay panting. Between gasps he said, 'Not - a - sausage. I must have picked the deepest part. I went down and down until I thought my lungs would bust but I didn't even touch bottom. If the box is down in that spot, we'll never lift it by ourselves! By the way, don't forget to swallow as you go down—not the seawater, though—because when you get deep the pressure makes your ears ache and swallowing will relieve them.'

He unhitched the rope which Jimmy tied round his own waist and then began to take a series of deep breaths, swelling and deflating his lungs in turn like bellows. Darcy watched him mystified and Jimmy explained, 'It's what they teach us in school. Something about storing up oxygen in your blood stream.'

'I'd settle for a jet motor,' said Darcy whose breathing was almost back to normal.

Jimmy poised lightly on his toes, then went over the edge in a neat dive. The water roared in his ears as he plunged down and the depths looked opaque, as though he were cutting his way through a golden-green fog. He swam on steadily, counting the strokes, six, seven, eight, nine. His pulse boomed inside his head and there was a piercing pain as the pressure increased on his ear drums. Suddenly, out of nowhere it seemed, the bottom tilted up towards him. He swam along it for a few strokes, peering through the gloom ahead. He could just make out the darker shadow of a pile of rocks and then he knew that his lungs were almost bursting. Red flashes darted in front of his eyes. He grabbed a handful of sand to prove that he had reached the bottom, then swung up sharply, up, up to the white surface. He seemed to be suspended in the milky atmosphere for ages and once he began to open his mouth to breath, certain that he must be clear by now. At last he clove the surface in a dazzling flash and air had never tasted sweeter to his tortured lungs. Still clutching his sand, he swam slowly to the side of the boat where strong hands heaved him aboard.

'You were gone for ages, Jim,' Jane said. 'It must have been the best part of a minute. I thought you were never coming up!'

He dropped the handful of sand on the planks and managed to gasp out between gulps of air, 'It's a terrible long way down. No sign of any box where I went but I did see some rocks ahead. If we could move the boat a bit that way, we'd have less distance to swim there and back.'

'Well done, Jimmy,' Darcy said. 'That's a bright idea.' He pulled in the anchor and between them they manœuvred the boat a few yards closer to the gigantic rock. 'Now then, Jane,' Darcy went on, 'your go. If you dive in at this angle, try to remember to keep to your right coming up. That'll take you well clear of the rocks and the boat. We don't want you banging your head on the bottom of the boat—you might damage the keel!'

She smiled at his joke and then dived over the side, the rope whipping out behind her. She was gone nearly as long as Jimmy and, like him, brought back a handful of sand as a trophy. From then on, they took it in turns, gradually quartering the floor of the sea and eliminating different areas in their search. They covered right in to the angle formed by the cliff side and the big rock and gradually a mosaic picture began to build itself bit by bit. The floor shelved steeply from the water's edge on the island side and there were a few scattered boulders resting on it just off the edge of the land. There was no sign of a chest or a box nearby and the water was too shallow and clear at this spot for them to miss a large rectangular object. The middle of the angle was open sand, which seemed too firm for even a heavy weight to have sunk right in. On their left, the side nearest the huge rock emerging from the sea, the water was deepest, dark and cold from the shadow cast by the rock itself. There were other, smaller rocks lying on the bottom alongside the big one, like piglets nestling against a sow, as Jane described it. They were probably chunks that the wind and the waves had over the centuries chipped away from the big rock. In fact, there was another great overhanging mass on the rock itself, formed by the sea which had carved away the softer stone at water-level, which seemed poised to crash down on their heads.

The three of them were tiring by the time they began to explore the area near the big rock. Jimmy had managed to penetrate the inky gloom a little way and he came up with a nasty graze on his left shin, having nearly jammed his leg by accident in a cleft between two boulders. Darcy decided to call it a day.

'We've done enough for the first time out,' he said. 'Dash it all, the time's flown—it's nearly three o'clock and the motor-boats will be back soon.'

'Must we stop now?' Jane asked. 'It's my turn. Can't I have just one last go?'

Darcy shook his head. ' 'Fraid not,' he answered. 'The salt's made your eyes quite red—and yours too, Jimmy. It'd be silly to go on too long and knock ourselves up. We'd only do less tomorrow. By the way, we simply must buy some diving masks and flippers when we get back. They'll make all the difference.'

'An underwater torch would help,' Jimmy added. 'It's as dark as a coal-hole down by the big rock there. If the treasure's anywhere, it must be round there. We've searched everywhere else.'

'Well, tomorrow we can concentrate on that area,' Darcy said. 'And maybe we can get hold of an underwater torch.'

'I wonder if anybody's ever invented one that straps round your forehead—like a miner's lamp?' Jane queried. 'That would be ideal because it would leave your hands free.'

'I bet Commander Cousteau or one of the real experts has thought of it already,' Darcy replied. 'If not, you can always patent it when we get back, Janey!'

They spent a few minutes tidying up the boat for the return journey and coiling the wet rope. Then Jimmy said, 'I wonder how the old Jacky's getting on? Last time I saw her she was paddling away past the corner there like the Oxford crew.' Jimmy was a Cambridge supporter!

'Heavens!' Darcy exclaimed. 'I'd forgotten all about Jacky for the time being! Better give her a yell.' He stood up in the boat and shouted at the top of his voice, 'Jacky! Jacky!'

There was no reply. The shore line looked deserted. They could not see round the corner Jimmy had mentioned, where he had last spotted Jacky. Darcy shouted again and this time the two Jays joined in but still there was no answering 'Cooee!'

'She is an ass sometimes,' Jimmy said. 'I bet she's tried to climb up the side of the cliff and got stuck.'

'In her bare feet?' Jane queried. 'Jacky's impetuous enough for most things but I can't see her trying to climb up through all that heathery stuff without shoes on. Her feet would be cut to ribbons before she'd gone a few yards.'

'Well, where is she then?' Jimmy asked irritably. 'I'm getting cold sitting here. Trust Jacky to keep us hanging around. She attracts trouble, the way a pot of jam attracts wasps!'

'What's that red thing floating into sight beyond the point?' said Darcy. 'Oh, it's only the dinghy. It gave me quite a fright for the moment.'

'Only the dinghy!' Jane exclaimed. 'What about Jacky?'

'She's probably lying flat in the bottom—trying to pull our legs and pretend it's floating away by itself,' came from Jimmy. 'You wait—in a moment she'll sit up.'

Jane shaded her eyes and peered anxiously across the sun-dappled sea. 'I don't think she's in it. It's bobbing about too much. Jacky's weight would make it ride deeper in the water.'

At that moment they heard splashing sounds behind the dinghy and then a yell that was abruptly cut off. Leaping up so that they nearly upset the boat, they could just see a dark head jerking along in the dinghy's wake.

'Gosh, it's Jacky!' shouted Jimmy. 'She's swimming after it!'

'She'll never make it,' Jane cried. 'She's way out of her depth and she can't swim that far! *She'll drown!*'

CHAPTER 7

Accidental or Deliberate?

THE same thought was leaping through Jacky's despairing mind. The exciting voyage of discovery had suddenly turned into a nightmare.

When she paddled away in the dinghy, she felt all the thrill of being given a responsible job to do on her own. There was the added attraction of exploring unknown territory. What a lark it would be, she thought, if the treasure chest happened to be hidden among the rocks by the water's edge and I found it single-handed while all the others were puffing and blowing about under the water by the big rock! She secretly envied them their swimming ability and wondered for the hundredth time why she could not match them despite all her efforts. She was just as strong as they were—well, as strong as Jane, anyway—and she put just as much energy into trying to swim. More energy, in fact. She fought the water, trying to hit and butt her way through it, while the others seemed quite lazy. Perhaps that was the secret, she suddenly thought—to relax and let the water help you instead of trying to fight it all the time. She must try out the theory when next she bathed.

By this time she had reached to within a yard or so of the water's edge. She felt the dinghy grate against a submerged rock and she paddled along gingerly. She would feel an awful fool if the dinghy got punctured and sank and the others had to rescue her. She moved along slowly, keeping a few feet away from the shore-line and she peered over the edge of the dinghy, her nose within six inches of the sea, trying to look down and spot the treasure chest if it happened to be washed up or dropped close in to the shore.

In this way Jacky slowly traced her way along parallel with the steep side of the island until she reached a finger of land that poked out into the sea. She paddled round this headland and found that the cliff on the far side curved away to form a small cove. The ground was much flatter on this side and there was a large slab of rock that met the sea at a gentle angle. Jacky decided to go ashore, realizing that she could search the coast-line better if she was free to stand erect and move about.

She dug the water with her paddle and drove the front of the dinghy up on to the flat rock. Then she scrambled out and, remembering what Darcy had said, lugged the dinghy clear of the sea to the top edge of the slab. It was wet and slippery with seaweed and once or twice she nearly slipped back with a splash but after much heaving and tugging she parked the dinghy six feet or more from the edge.

She found a couple of stones, each as big as a brick, and wedged them underneath the dinghy. There, she thought, standing back and studying her handi-work, that can't budge now.

She wandered along the coast-line. The rocky edge was not only greasy in places with dank sea-weed but encrusted with limpets as well and Jacky picked her way delicately. The pools and shallow basins between the submerged rocks were alive with small fishes. She stopped to watch a pointed shell apparently moving along under its own steam. Then she noticed two small claws gently emerging and scrabbling at the sand. It was a hermit crab, creeping along to the shelter of an underwater ledge. In a deeper pool nearby she saw a sudden commotion and when the water cleared, she spotted a strange greyish object suspended in the limpid depths. It was rather like a jellyfish but it had longer tentacles and a round eye that seemed to stare back at her. For some moments it stayed motionless and then it darted across the pool by contracting and jerking out its tentacles in a kind of jet propulsion. Jacky recalled the natural history books she had read and realized suddenly with a shiver of horror that it was a baby octopus. She looked again at the trailing tentacles and shuddered. I wouldn't like to have those slimy things fastening on to my ankle when I was paddling, she thought. Nor meet your big brother, my boy! She picked up a pebble and flung it into the water. The baby octopus shot away, covering its departure with a squirt of blackish liquid that stained the clear pool for several minutes afterwards. Good riddance, Jacky thought.

For the next half hour she patrolled the rugged beach to the far side of the cove and back. However diligently she scrutinized it, there was not a trace of the German officer's loot. The sun beat down fiercely and she could feel it, almost like a physical weight, on her bare shoulders and neck. No breeze crept into the landlocked cove and Jacky felt drowsy and a little light-headed from the heat of the sun. Retracing her steps back to the rubber dinghy, which was almost red hot to the touch, she found a smooth patch of sand, just large enough for her to lie down on. I'll rest for a bit, she thought. They're bound to give me a shout if they want to move off. She lay back and closed her eyes but even then there was a red glow behind the lids from the fierce sunshine. She wriggled into a comfortable position. A few minutes later, she was fast asleep.

She awoke with a start after about an hour. She had had a horrible dream in which a wild animal with eight tentacles instead of legs came scrambling down the cliffside above and tore the dinghy to shreds. In the dream Jacky had tried to jump up but her limbs were weighted down and she could only struggle slowly into a sitting position all the while that the creature, which had only one eye in the middle of its head, methodically destroyed the dinghy.

She sat up with a jerk, rubbed her eyes and looked round. The dinghy had gone from the nearby rock! Startled, she swung her head and stared up the cliff, half-expecting to see this weird creature of her dream disappearing into the trees. She thought she heard a rustle in the undergrowth but decided she was imagining things. By this time she was on her feet, swinging her head wildly from side to side. And then she saw the dinghy, floating serenely in the sea some fifteen feet from the shore. Even as she watched it aghast, it bobbed another foot or two further away. The paddle was still inboard where she had left it.

Jacky felt guilty. She couldn't understand why but, somehow or another, it must have slipped down the rock and into the sea in spite of her precautions. But that's nonsense, she thought. I wedged it firmly with the stones. It just couldn't have climbed by itself over the stones and walked into the water. She glanced swiftly at the slab of the rock. The stones were still there but she distinctly remembered having placed them almost touching each other. Now they were a good three feet apart. Some-one must have come along when I was asleep, she thought, and deliberately pushed the dinghy into the sea!

By this time the little boat had floated a few more

feet away from her. She seemed rooted to the spot, unable to decide what to do. Caution urged her to yell out to Darcy and the others, who could easily swim round the headland and catch the dinghy before it went much further. But pride warned her of the teasing she would get from them. Good old Jacky, they would laugh, typical, isn't it? She goes off to sleep and lets the dinghy float away under her nose. Had a good sleep, Jacky, you dozy creature? they would say.

No, she was jolly well going to get the dinghy herself! She could wade part of the way out to it and swim the rest. So, clenching her teeth, Jacky stepped down into the sea and began to thread her path between the slippery underwater rocks. A tremor slid coldly across her shoulders. She hoped fervently that the senior members of the octopus family had taken the day off.

She was up to her waist in the sea and still the dinghy bobbed and beckoned to her a few yards ahead. Suddenly her foot plunged into space as the shore fell away and she went under. She came up, spluttering and coughing and gave an involuntary yell. Then she began to strike out doggedly towards the little boat. I mustn't panic, she thought to herself. Ten strokes ought to do it and I know I can swim ten strokes. She began to count silently, two, three, four, five, six. She tried to follow Darcy's instructions, breathing slowly through her nose and not scrambling her movements. Once or twice a wave slapped her in the face and she swallowed a mouthful of salt water which nearly made her retch. She was beginning to tire and still the dinghy seemed just as far away as ever, enticing her on. It had reached the cross-current beyond the headland and it swirled to her left, drifting faster towards the open sea. Jacky could feel the current tugging at her leaden arms and legs. She was wallowing lower in the water now and at every other breath she seemed to take in a mouthful of salt. Still she swam on, mechanically pushing her arms in front of her, thirteen, fourteen, fifteen strokes. She was almost at the end of her tether and a red sheen hung in front of her eyes. It was all she could do now to keep her head clear of the waves and even so she was shipping water, swallowing more with each gasp. She no longer had control of her limbs. Her legs sank lower, the current pulling them down. Almost as though she were watching the antics of somebody else, Jacky felt herself going under. The sea roared in her ears and she knew, almost impersonally, that this was the end.

Then, suddenly, strong hands grabbed her and she found herself hauled up into the precious air. Darcy had arrived. With a few powerful strokes he hauled her back to the shore, lifted her clear of the submerged rocks and gently laid her down on the patch of sand where she had slept a little while before.

He began to press rhythmically against the small of her back, beneath the lower ribs, and the foul-tasting salt started to pump out of her lungs. She coughed and spat and with every racking breath she felt better.

Jimmy had swum after the dinghy which he now towed back to the shore. When Jacky was fit enough to move, they placed her in it and, with Jimmy paddling and Darcy swimming at the side helping it along, they soon had her back in the sailing boat.

She recovered quickly and seemed none the worse for her frightening experience. The boat was scudding back towards Alassio when she was fit enough to talk normally.

'I know what you're all thinking,' she said quietly, 'although you're too nice to say it. You think I disobeyed instructions and let the dinghy float off, don't you? Well, I didn't—really I didn't.' She went on to describe how she had hauled the dinghy high up on the rock and had wedged it with a couple of stones; and how the stones had been moved apart when she saw the dinghy in the sea.

They all knew that Jacky was completely honest. She might be impetuous and get into scrapes but she wouldn't lie her way out of any blame. Jimmy said tentatively, 'Perhaps the stones shifted under the weight of the dinghy and slipped down the rock?'

Jacky shook her head firmly. 'No, they couldn't have. I remember clearly wedging them into a tiny ledge on the rock. And anyway the dinghy wouldn't be anything like as heavy as the stones. You saw them, Dashitall—they were about the size of a brick each. It was all I could do to lift them with one hand.'

'What's the alternative?' Jimmy asked. 'Either the wind blew them apart or they shifted under their own weight. You're not suggesting someone came along when you were asleep and deliberately chucked the dinghy into the sea?'

'I can't see any other answer,' Jacky replied. 'Actually, I thought I heard a rustle in the bushes above when I was just waking up but at the time I thought no more about it. Now I'm beginning to wonder.'

Jane cut in eagerly. 'That reminds me,' she said. 'When we were bringing the boat close in, I had the impression someone was watching us from the island—remember? I had the definite sensation of being spied on.'

'That was just your imagination,' said her brother. 'You're always imagining things—like thinking you're a better rider than I am, for instance!'

Jane stuck out her tongue at him. Darcy, sitting at the tiller, summed up by saying, 'There might be something in that theory. Probably some local kid playing on the island thought it would be a great joke to maroon Jacky. I'd like to up-end him over my knee—if it is so! I'd teach him to fool around with other people's boats—and nearly their lives!'

'I never thanked you properly for saving me, Dashitall,' Jacky said.

He went even redder underneath his lobster-like complexion. 'All in the day's work,' he replied airily. 'Anyway, I'll touch your papa for a handsome reward!'

'If it was a local kid fooling around,' Jane persisted, 'do you think he'll give the game away? Us diving for the treasure, I mean.'

'I doubt it,' Darcy said. 'No one else really knows about the treasure—and you know what they say about mad dogs and Englishmen. The Eye-ties think all foreigners are crazy. If the tale got round about us diving, the locals would only put it down to a peculiar form of midsummer madness, I reckon!'

By this time they had sailed the boat back to the yacht basin where they berthed her and arranged to hire her again next day. Then they climbed wearily into Bertha, who had been waiting patiently all day, and drove slowly back to the hotel along the shore road. They were pleasantly tired and hungry. Even Jacky, who claimed that she ought to have three extra meals a day for the next week—to make up for all she had brought up after her swimming experience!

When they had showered and changed their clothes, Darcy suggested they should go out and

[155]

have tea at an open-air café and then buy some diving gear at the shop in the Drain. 'Don't forget we've only got two more clear days,' he said, 'tomorrow and Friday, before we have to drive back to Cannes. We can't afford to waste any time.'

'Couldn't we stay a day or two longer, Darcy?' Jane pleaded. 'We've never had a holiday like this before!'

''Fraid not,' he said. 'I'd love to stay for months but I've got to report back for duty next week. Besides, I've got my ticket booked for the ferry plane on Monday night and it'll take me all my time to get back to Le Touquet by then. Also, don't forget Jacky's father. He hasn't seen her for weeks and he'll be arriving in Cannes on Saturday. No, if we don't find any treasure by Friday afternoon, we've had it—at least for this year.'

They strolled along to the nearest square and for the next half hour the Three Jays gorged themselves on gooey cakes while Darcy hid behind a copy of yesterday's paper, catching up with the cricket scores. Then Jimmy nudged his arm, saying softly, 'D'you see that man sitting three tables away? The one with the black glove on his left hand. I'll swear I've seen him somewhere before!'

Darcy glanced up. He recognized the German who had stood near them on the ramparts of the Gallinara fort the previous afternoon. The man sat gazing out to sea but Darcy had the queer sensation that he was secretly watching them. He was not lolling in his chair, relaxed and unconcerned. He sat stiffly upright and his damaged left hand in the black glove seemed to be tensed, ready to spring into action at once.

Darcy shook his head. Next thing he would start getting one of Jane's fancies and imagine they were being spied on. He answered Jimmy casually, 'Oh yes, we've certainly seen him before. He was up at the fort on the island yesterday the same time we were.'

'Oh, that's it,' Jimmy said. 'I knew I'd seen him somewhere. Tough-looking character, isn't he?'

'Not too loud, Jim,' said Darcy, nudging his elbow. 'It's not only English people who can speak English, you know. He might overhear you. Well, how about getting on with our shopping? Dash it all, it's gone half past six and we'll have to get a move on.'

He paid the bill and then they sauntered across the square, dodging between tables and cars that were parked in a higgledy-piggledy way. Jimmy paused to admire a sleek red Alfa Romeo with the words 'Sprint Veloce' scrawled in chromium script across the back.

'Some bus,' he said. 'I bet she can shift.'

Jacky piped up, 'How about swopping Bertha for that one, Dashitall?'

'Shame on you,' he replied. 'That's almost

sacrilege. Besides, we'd never fit all you lumps into a thing like that. That's the worst of these streamlined jobs. They're fine for two people but you'd need a family of legless dwarfs to seat any more in comfort. No, give me Bertha any day!' Nevertheless, he gave an envious backward look at the Alfa as they passed on.

Before long they came to the shop that sold the diving gear and also displayed coloured postcards, toys and souvenirs of Alassio. They paused to inspect the flippers and masks that were hung in a bundle outside the door. 'If we could buy a pair of flippers that would fit the three of us,' said Darcy, 'we could make do with just the one pair.' He was becoming conscious of the fact that his stock of Italian lire was not elastic and there would be a sizeable hotel bill to settle in a couple of days' time.

Jane glanced down at his sandalled feet and giggled. They looked enormous compared to her own. 'If we got a pair to fit you,' she replied, 'we could cut out hiring the boat tomorrow. We'd only need to put a sail on one flipper and Jimmy and I could get out to the island on that!'

Darcy gave her a playful shove. 'Nothing wrong with my feet,' he said.

'Nothing at all,' Jimmy agreed. 'But mind you, no one would ever nickname you Cinderella!'

'Any policemen in the family?' Jane asked.

Darcy decided to ignore them and change the

subject. 'There's no point in us buying one of those schnorkel tubes with a pingpong ball at the top end. They're only for cruising along with your noggin just under the surface. I wonder if they sell real masks and oxygen cylinders to strap on your back?'

'No sign of them,' Jimmy said, looking all round the crowded window. 'Anyway, wouldn't they be a bit complicated for us? We'd need a real expert to show us how to work them.'

'Aren't you a real expert, Dashitall?' enquired Jane, a shade maliciously.

'In most things, yes,' he answered. 'But on this one occasion—alas, no.'

'Well, I vote we settle for something straight-forward,' Jimmy said. 'We know we can dive to the bottom out by the rock. All we want is a bit of extra help and something to keep the salt out of our eyes.'

Jacky had been unusually silent but now she interrupted their discussion. 'I think that man's following us,' she said softly. 'The one who sat near us just now. I've been watching him while you were talking and he stood quite close a moment ago, pretending to look at that rack of postcards. There he is—by the newspaper stand.'

Jimmy laughed at her eagerness. 'Go on,' he said. 'Next thing you'll say he's Hitler with his moustache shaved off! It's a free country—nothing to stop him doing his shopping same time as us.'

'But he's not buying anything,' Jacky persisted.

'Nor are we—with all this arguing,' was Jimmy's quick retort. 'Anyway, he's going now,' he added, as the man began to walk away.

They trooped into the shop and managed to make the smiling woman-owner understand what they wanted. After trying on different sizes of flippers, they finally settled for a large pair for Darcy and a smaller pair that would fit Jimmy or Jane equally well. They also bought two circular face masks with a plastic window that fitted over the eyes and nose. The woman tried to sell them a diving knife and a kind of blowpipe affair that fired a dart by a powerful spring. They were tempted and, as Jane remarked, 'It would make wonderful camouflage,' but finally Darcy decided that it would be an expensive way of putting any suspicious person off the scent. They did, however, buy a waterproof torch.

It was getting dusk as they walked back towards the hotel, clutching their purchases. They passed the Grand Hotel with its gay lights and visitors sitting out on the veranda sipping aperitifs. The Drain narrowed again for the last part of the walk and there was only just room for the four of them to walk abreast with a high wall on their left and a row of tall houses on their right. Jacky was on the left, then Darcy, then Jimmy and Jane. The last two were as usual teasing Darcy while Jacky was surprisingly quiet, perhaps from the delayed result of her adventures a few hours before.

Suddenly there was a roaring noise behind them, that seemed to bounce off the walls and smother them in a crescendo of sound. Darcy, with the split-second reactions of a pilot, leapt into motion. He shoved Jimmy and Jane sprawling in a heap against the side of the houses and, almost in the same swift movement, half-lifted, half-pulled himself and Jacky flat against the opposite wall. A big black car rushed by without lights, then the driver flicked on his headlights, slowed down with a squealing of brakes, swung at right angles round a corner thirty yards ahead and disappeared.

Jimmy and Jane picked themselves up and began to dust down their shorts. Jane found herself trembling and Jimmy gazed ruefully at a tear on the left leg of his shorts where the wing of the car had just grazed him as it whipped past. 'Talk of road-hogs . . .' he began.

'That was no road-hog,' Darcy interrupted grimly. 'That was deliberate!'

'What?' they said in chorus.

'Yes,' he went on, picking his words slowly. 'I can't think why but that joker meant to hit us. The Italians fancy themselves as fast drivers but they aren't crazy. Haven't you noticed how they sound their hooters at every road junction and bend? Even if the driver had been tight—and that would be rare at this time of night—he would have had his lights on and his hooter blaring away. That so-and-so deliberately crept up on us. He must have got up speed, cut his engine and coasted along until he was twenty or thirty yards away, then shoved her into third and accelerated.'

'That's the second time in one day you've saved my life,' Jacky said to Darcy, rather shakily. 'If you hadn't been so quick, he'd have mowed us all down. I just hope you don't get the chance of making it a habit!'

'I'd like to have five minutes alone with him in some quiet spot,' Darcy muttered through clenched teeth, almost to himself. 'Pity we didn't have time to see who it was.'

'I think I did,' said Jane.

'You—what?'

'Yes. When you pushed me and Jimmy against the house, I caught a glimpse of him reflected in a window. Mind you, he was gone in a flash and I wouldn't swear to it. But I'd say it was the same man we'd seen before—the one with the bad hand!'

CHAPTER 8

Sea-horse

WHEN the four of them assembled for break-fast next morning, they were greeted with an unexpected sight. Instead of clear blue skies and the hot sunlight dancing on the waves, there were dark rainclouds looming over the sea which reared and tossed, sending huge white-crested waves thumping on the beach. Rain scudded against the windows of the dining room.

Darcy summed up all their private fears when he said, 'That's torn it. No trip to the island today unless it clears up—and Luigi in the hotel here told me that this weather's in for the day!'

'Come to sunny Alassio,' Jacky said. 'I don't think! I feel terribly cheated.'

'That's not really fair,' Darcy answered her. 'The weather's been lovely so far and you've got to expect the odd bad day now it's near the end of August.'

'Well, why couldn't it wait till next week after we've gone?' she retorted. 'Don't you think we might chance it?'

'Not a hope. You can't even see the island from here. We're not good enough sailors to get the boat out of harbour on a day like this. Anyway, you can bet that the waves are pounding the rocks out there. They'll be churning up so much muck and sand that you couldn't see a sausage under water.'

They ate their breakfast despondently and then gathered in the lounge. Before long the conversation came round to the near-disaster of the night before and they discussed it from all angles. It was a frightening thought that someone unknown to them hated them so much that he would attempt to commit murder—unless he happened to be a sheer lunatic. And, if Jane was correct, that someone was the German with the damaged hand.

'That's what beats me,' Jimmy remarked. 'Why? Why should he pick on us? Apart from the fact we've seen him just once before—on the island—he's a complete stranger. We've never done anything to him. There's no rhyme or reason to it.'

'Wait a sec, Jimmy,' Jane said eagerly. 'The penny's dropping—I think I see a connection. Let's take it in order.' She held up her left hand, fingers spread, and began ticking them off with her right forefinger as she went on, 'First, we see him on the island. Second, I get the feeling we're being spied on—and that could have been him.'

'It could have been one of ten thousand people in Alassio—if it happened at all,' Jimmy commented sourly.

'Hold it, Jim,' said Darcy. 'Let her say her piece.'

'As I was saying when I was rudely interrupted,'

Jane grinned, 'third, someone pushes the dinghy into the sea when Jacky's asleep—and that could be him again. Fourth, we definitely see him watching us over tea and then he follows us to the shop with the diving kit. Fifth, he nips off, gets his car—which looked like a German Mercedes to me—and tries to bump us off. There is a connection behind all that.'

'Too many ifs and buts for me,' Jimmy grunted. 'Anyway, let's buy it. Supposing for the sake of argument, there is a connection—what is it?'

'This,' she answered. 'He's got a bad hand, remember. The one with the black glove on it. Now when Dashitall told us the story at breakfast time about the German commander and the loot, he mentioned one little point that stuck in my mind. It was about the second-in-command who got left behind and who fought it out in the mountains when the Allies closed in. Do you remember now—*Darcy said he got wounded in the hand!*'

'Dash it all!' Darcy exclaimed.

'Now do you see the connection,' Jane rushed on. 'Let's suppose for a moment that this man with the bad hand is really the second-in-command. As far as he knows, no one else has a clue about the loot. The commander and all the U-boat crew are dead and the local people never knew about it anyway. He comes back to Alassio and goes out to the island as a tourist but really to have a good look round.

Then he happens to see us there. Nothing strange in that. But next day, when he's there having a private snoop, we turn up with a boat and start diving. At once he knows we're on to something. So he tries to scare us off by faking an accident with the dinghy. He probably guessed that Jacky—begging your pardon, Jay—wasn't a terribly strong swimmer. Anyway, we get out of that all right, so then he trails us when we arrive back and sees us buying flippers and masks. He knows now that we mean business. So he has to get tougher and tries to mow us down in his car. If he'd only hit just one of us, he would guess that the rest would pack up the holiday and leave the field clear for him. Couldn't that be the answer?'

'Sounds fair enough to me,' Darcy said.

'Wait a moment,' Jimmy interrupted. 'If I remember right, you said, Darcy, that the second-in-command was sent to prison as a war criminal. You mentioned he got fifteen years, I think it was. Well, it's not fifteen years since the war. He'd still have several years to go.'

'There's such a thing as remission of sentence for good conduct,' Darcy replied. 'Besides, a lot of minor war criminals have been released in the last few years. No, Jim, I don't think you can rule him out on those grounds.'

'Aren't we being a bit casual,' Jacky said. 'Here we are sitting around and coolly discussing a desperate character who's used to knocking people off and who looks like adding us to the list!'

'What do you want us to do?' Jane demanded. 'Go to the local police station and say, "Please, sir, we think someone's trying to kill us"? We'd have to have some real proof and so far this is just theory. And if we went to the police, we'd have to tell them all about the treasure.'

'We're safe enough in daylight, I think,' Darcy said. 'He may be desperate but he's not going to risk anything too obvious. The thing is not to wander around any of these quiet back-alleys on our own but always stick together. Anyway, there's only tomorrow left—and he'd hardly follow us out of Italy.'

'Only tomorrow,' Jimmy repeated with a sigh. 'We've just got to find the treasure tomorrow!'

*　　*　　*

Friday arrived, their last full day in Alassio. The storm had spent itself and dawn broke on another golden day. The Jays and Darcy were up early and into the dining room as soon as it opened. By a quarter past eight they were setting out for the yacht basin in Bertha. Jane had rooted round to find a needle and thread with which she cobbled up the rip in Jimmy's one pair of shorts. This was the only sign that someone had tried to run them down on Wednesday evening. The bright sunshine on their

M

[167]

faces as they drove along the coast road seemed to make their fears and theories evaporate, just as it was drying up the thin wisps of mist on the calm surface of the sea. There was no trace anywhere of the German with the damaged hand; Jimmy, in fact, started to tease Jane for being fanciful.

Darcy parked Bertha in the shade of a nearby wall and they began to unload their picnic lunch, the dinghy, the flippers and the mask. The Three Jays had each acquired a fine tan through days of exposure to the sun and the wind. Darcy thought they made a wonderful picture of health, teeth gleaming white in an expanse of sunburn as they laughed and joked with one another on their way along the little jetty. He even glanced smugly at his own long limbs which were beginning to turn a shade of pinkish brown underneath the mass of freckles. Whether they found any treasure or not, they would still have one or two mementoes to take back from Alassio, he thought—and not least the experience of a marvellous holiday.

They sailed out past the island and repeated the routine of Wednesday by eating their picnic lunch while they waited for the motor-boat loads of tourists to leave Gallinara. They were all impatient to get on and it seemed ages before the hands of Darcy's watch crawled round to half past twelve and the motor-boats departed with much tooting on their sirens. Just as Darcy was raising the sail, a speedboat went zooming past fifty yards further out to sea, the pilot hunched over the wheel. Their sailing boat rocked and bounced in the spreading wake and Darcy had to grab the mast hurriedly to stop himself pitching overboard. 'That was a bit unnecessary,' he grunted. 'Got the whole sea to himself and he has to shoot past us like that!'

'Do you think it might have been Jane's pal?' asked Jimmy, a shade maliciously.

'Pooh,' said Jane.

'I doubt it,' Darcy answered, 'just some road-hog —or sea-hog would be better—I reckon. That reminds me. If it is Jane's pal, as you call him, we'd better get a move on. It's just struck me that all he'd have to do is ram us amidships travelling at speed —and that would be the end of our adventure!'

'Gosh, I never thought of that,' Jacky exclaimed.

'It would be only too easy for him,' Darcy went on. 'And he could always make out it had been an accident—that we sailed across his path too late for him to swerve. There are no witnesses to prove otherwise and, if any one of us did manage to struggle back to land, it'd only be our word against his. Let's get moving! The sooner we're in the shelter of the island, the better I'll like it!'

'You're such a comfort, Dashitall,' Jane remarked. 'You think of the nicest things!'

As the boat swung on to its new course, they kept glancing surreptitiously in the direction where the speedboat had disappeared, half-expecting to see it charging at them. As Jimmy said, it was rather like walking across a field where there may be an angry bull knocking around. But there was no sign or sound of the speedboat and they dismissed it as just another example of Italian love for speed and reckless driving.

Darcy dropped anchor close under the huge rock, a few feet nearer the one patch that they had not combed thoroughly two days before. The sun was almost overhead and it cast a deep purple shadow across the mysterious depths. The mass of overhanging grey rock which they had noticed on the earlier trip seemed to loom over the place where the treasure might be lying. Jacky shuddered quietly. There was an eerie sensation about the deathly hush and the strange stillness of the secret water. It rose and fell with its own private pulse of tide and to her tensed-up imagination, the sea was almost like the flank of some wild beast, heaving gently but menacingly as it lapped against the grimly towering rock. Her eyes kept straying in spite of herself to the cove not fifty yards away where she had almost drowned forty-eight hours before.

Darcy broke into her thoughts by saying, 'Right now—down to business. Same order as before, me first, then Jimmy, then Jane. Remember, we're nearer than ever to the rock so watch out and don't forget which side is the open one. Keep enough breath in reserve to get up safely and always come up outwards away from the rock. That quite clear?'

Jimmy and Jane nodded but Jacky said, 'What about me?'

'Oh, I've got a special job for you,' Darcy replied. 'You're O.C. diving operations. Look, here's a rough sketch I drew last night.' He produced a piece of paper from his shorts pocket and a stub of pencil. 'It's not to scale, of course, but here's the rough line of the rock under water and I've shaded in lightly where we think there are other bits of rock under water. You'd better watch this, Jimmy and Jane, because this is the plan.' They crowded round and Darcy went on, 'We'll take it methodically, starting at this end—here—and working right along towards the corner. We'll each take a rock in turn and try to swim all round it, looking at all the cracks and crevices. Then, when we come up, we'll describe it to Jacky who will draw the outline on the sketch. Before each one dives, he must take a look at the map and try to memorize it. That way, we won't waste our time—if we're lucky!—by exploring a rock under water that someone else has already checked. Do you follow me?'

'Yes,' they said.

'So, Jacky, I've given you quite a job there. I'm relying on you!'

Darcy tied the rope end round his waist, wriggled his toes into the large pair of flippers and then took the mask and dipped it in the sea, sloshing the water round inside it before tipping out the spare drops.

'What on earth are you doing that for?' Jane demanded. 'I thought the idea was to keep your face and eyes dry—not the reverse!'

'That's an old trick,' Darcy replied loftily. 'All real experts know it. If you don't wet the inside of the mask first, it's liable to steam up and then you're worse off than without it. Here goes!'

He pulled the mask on over his face, just leaving his mouth and chin clear. He took a few deep breaths, then flapped like a penguin to the stern of the boat, raised his arms and dived in with a splash.

'Gosh, he's forgotten the torch,' Jimmy exclaimed.

'Real experts don't need one,' said Jane a little tartly.

Darcy seemed to be gone for ages. When he finally burst up through the placid surface, Jacky said he looked like 'The Thing From Outer Space'—with his sandy hair trailing like seaweed all round the mask. He swam over to the side of the boat and hauled himself in.

Rather breathlessly, he said, 'This gear makes all the difference. I reckon I reached the bottom in three or four strokes. But you've got to remember not to try a breast-stroke kick with the flippers. The thing to do is give little up-and-down kicks with your feet—a sort of crawl kick.'

'Well, did you find anything?' Jane asked.

Darcy paused from tugging the lobe of one ear to clear the water out, grinned and said, 'Not a sausage. But I did check the whole of the first rock. Listen, you others, while I try to describe it to Jacky for her sketch.'

When he had finished, Jimmy, who had already donned the other pair of flippers and had wetted the inside of the spare mask, tied the rope round his waist and shuffled over to the stern of the boat. He went through his deep breathing routine and hopped over the side.

He quickly realized that Darcy was right. The flippers and the mask made a big difference. He seemed to glide through the water and there was no longer the smarting pressure of the salt on his eyeballs. He drove on through the greeny-grey depths and touched bottom just short of the first jagged boulder which he recognized from the description as 'Darcy's rock'. He edged past it and began to search its neighbour, which was rounded and slippery with weeds that lifted, tendril-like, to the motion of his strokes. He managed to wriggle his way between it and the wall of rock that rose sheer out of the water but found nothing. Then he half-swam, half-crawled over its smooth top and investigated the open side. A large fish suddenly darted from cover right in front of his mask and the shock nearly made him open his mouth and shout. Luckily, the fish seemed the more frightened of the two and it shot away. A shade scared in case its mate was in the area, Jimmy grimly continued his search until the pain in his lungs and the red flashes jumping in front of his eyes warned him to break off and make for the surface. It was only when his face was clear and he was gratefully gulping in fresh air that he remembered he was still gripping the rubber torch in his left hand—and had quite forgotten to switch it on when he was under water!

He clambered aboard and told the others of his experiences. Jacky outlined the second rock on her plan and Jane studied it before she dived in turn.

They each completed a second dive and had now worked their way quite near the angle of the big rock and the edge of the island without finding a thing. Darcy went down for the third time and Jimmy followed him. Still nothing to report—except more boulders and seaweed. By this stage they realized that they were wasting precious breath in having to swim a long way under water past rocks they had already searched. So Darcy hauled up the anchor and paddled the boat several yards nearer their present area of search. They also decided to dispense with the rope round their waists. It was liable to catch on the submerged rocks and get tangled with their legs as they turned and twisted.

When the boat was anchored in its new station, Jane's third dive was to take place. The spot where she dived was in the darkest shadow of all and she disappeared into a pool of ink once the surface splash had subsided. There was now no rope snaking out to show the watchers in the boat that she was moving about far below them. Darcy wondered secretly whether he had been wise to dispense with it. Jane might have vanished into space for all he could see and if she got into difficulties down there, it might be impossible to find her.

The seconds ticked by and each one was an age to Darcy's anxious mind. He began to tense his limbs, ready to spring overboard to her rescue if she failed to come up within another ten seconds. Jimmy caught his eye and he tried to grin back but it was a feeble effort. And then, just as he was half-on his feet, there was a commotion below the placid surface and Jane's head and shoulders shot clear, only a yard or so from the side of the boat. Darcy leant out, grabbed her and tugged her over the side. She was silent for a moment, drawing in great gulps of air and then she shouted, 'I've found it! I've found it!' She waved a hoop of slimy rope in her right hand.

They clustered round, all yelling questions at her. Darcy shouted at the other two and finally quietened them. 'Dash it all,' he roared, 'let the girl speak! She can't hear herself think for all your noise.'

Jane still clutched the piece of rope, as the others fell silent. Then she gabbled, 'It's there! It really is. But the box has bust open. It's gone rotten from being under water all this time. Look—here's one of the handles. I gave it a tug to see if I could shift the box and it came away in my hand.'

'Where's the chest?' Jimmy demanded.

'Yes, tell us,' asked Jacky, her eyes glowing with excitement.

'Give her a chance,' Darcy said. They spoke almost simultaneously, so that Jane could hardly catch a distinct word. But she sensed the drift of their questions and went on, 'At the far side almost in the corner, it gets terribly deep. There are two rocks like pillars side by side with a gap between them. The box is wedged a few feet down in the gap but it must have got banged a lot because one side seems to be split right open.'

'I bet most of the treasure has spilt out,' Jimmy said. 'Can you swim down between the two rocks?'

'I doubt it,' Jane replied, shaking her head. 'The gap between them isn't much more than a foot or two.'

'Anyway, some of the bigger stuff may have got stuck in the box or between the rocks,' Darcy said. 'Though I reckon those old paintings and things won't be improved after being all this time in salt water!'

'Let's go and see,' Jimmy suggested. 'We're wasting time talking!'

'Half a mo',' said Darcy. 'The stuff has been there for over ten years. It can wait another minute or

[177]

two. Now, Jane, can you describe exactly where you found it?'

She could and she did. Darcy dived and came back to confirm her words. The box was indeed there, wedged between the rocks. He thought it was about five feet by three feet and it was tipped on one side. It was too firmly stuck to be shifted by a heave and he decided that the only solution was to try to fasten a rope round it and for all of them to tug it up from the boat.

The excitement of actually finding the treasure-chest spurred them on and everyone worked with a will. When each had dived twice more they had managed to work the rope end round the box and tie it with a double reef-knot. Then they had a brief council of war.

'May I suggest something?' Jimmy asked. When Darcy nodded, he went on, 'If we all pull on the rope, it might slip off the box and we'd be back where we started. I vote that one of us swims down and helps guide the box.'

'Good idea, Jim,' Darcy replied. 'I like that. You'd better go down because you can stay under longest. But for Heaven's sake, keep clear of the rope. We don't want to heave you up as well! We'll give you a few seconds to arrive and then we'll start pulling.'

Darcy gently took the strain until the rope was taut. Jacky and Jane stood in line behind him, each gripping the rope and alert to start tugging. Darcy counted 'One-two-three-go!' aloud and then they began to heave.

Suddenly there was a rumble from high above their heads. A great boulder came bouncing and tumbling down the side of the island cliff, leapt into space and hung blackly over them for a split second. Then it landed in the sea, not ten yards away. A fountain of water rose behind it and the splashes spattered the side of the boat.

'Ye Gods!' exclaimed Darcy. 'What was that?'

A second boulder, even bigger, followed it and a third. This last one was near the mark. It crashed like thunder against the steep rock and dropped into the pool close to where Jimmy had dived. It had smacked fair and square against the overhanging arch of rock. There was an ominous creak and a rumble, which Jacky later described as like standing in a tunnel when an express roars past. Then tons of rock came tumbling down into the sea making the water boil and hiss.

'Jimmy'll be killed!' shrieked Jane. The others stood aghast, as the boat jerked violently to and fro under the impact of the tossing waves. Jane sprang to the side of the boat but Darcy gently restrained her. In one stark flash he knew that nothing could save Jimmy if he were underneath that mass of stone.

But then Jacky gave a shrill squeak and pointed. Jimmy bobbed up, pale with shock, and feebly pawed the water. Darcy leapt in, grabbed his shoulders and helped him aboard. In a trice he had the anchor up and drove the boat away with fierce strokes on the oars. A fourth rock came bounding down the side of the cliff and spouted in the pool just where they had been a moment before, but it was too late. Darcy had already forced a twenty-yard gap between the pool and the boat. Still, he went on rowing until they were two or three hundred yards clear of the island. He shipped the oars, hoisted the mainsail and relaxed with a sigh.

Jimmy was recovering and at last was able to talk. 'Whew-w-w!' he said slowly. 'I don't want anything closer than that!'

'What happened, Jim?' asked Jacky.

'I don't really know. One moment I was down there by the box and the next I thought an earthquake had struck. I just managed to push off to one side and it felt as though someone was shaking me up and down. I just can't describe it. What really happened?'

'There was a landslide, Jim,' Jane said.

Darcy broke silence. 'That was no landslide,' he said quietly. 'That was our German friend's doing. I caught a glimpse of him high up on the cliff when that last boulder came down. He levered it off with a big stick!'

'The beast!' Jacky exclaimed. 'Are you going to report him to the police when we get back?'

SEA-HORSE

Darcy gave a weary shrug. 'What's the use?
He'd only deny it and it would be our word against
his. The clever swine!'

'So we just let him get away with attempted
murder?'

'Well,' said Darcy, 'he didn't succeed—thank God!
And if we'll never find the treasure now, nor will he!
You'd need thousands of pounds worth of machinery
and drilling tools to get through all those tons of rock
on top of it. So, in mucking us, he's mucked himself—and a jolly good job, too!'

Jacky looked back with a sigh at the island of
Gallinara, now dwindling in the distance. 'So that's
the last we'll ever see of the treasure,' she said wistfully.

Jimmy broke silence. 'Not quite the last. I did
find this on a ledge just by the broken box.' He
opened his fist which had been clenched tight and
displayed a small bronze statue of a horse, green with
age and crusted from its years in the sea. They
crowded round to gaze at it and Darcy made a close
inspection. 'Boy, it might be valuable,' he said. 'I
saw a picture in a book of Etruscan statuettes and
there was one of a horse quite like that.' He paused
and then summed up the whole adventure in one
sentence. 'Trust you Three Jays,' he said. 'The
whole sea to dive in and you have to come up with
a horse!'

*　　*　　*

And that is really the end of my story. Next day Darcy drove the Three Jays back across the Italian frontier to Cannes, where they joined Jacky's father on the yacht and had still more fun. After a lot of heart-searching and discussion, they decided to declare the bronze horse when they reached the Italian customs at Menton. They explained that they had found it in the sea—which was quite true— and the customs official gave a smile and a shrug and let them through with it.

As I write these last words, the little statue, now cleaned and polished, stands on the desk before me, a memento to an exciting holiday in Alassio. As Darcy remarked, trust the Three Jays to go diving and come back with a horse!

THE END